The Hunter

***

The Hideaway Series

Book 1

By: Mary Reason Theriot

Dedication

Without the love and support of my family, I would not have ventured to attempt and write this book.

Theresa, thank you so much for encouraging me to write a book. Without you, this book would never have come to fruition.   We had some great bonding time in the process also.

To my wonderful husband, without your help and support this book would never have been completed. If nothing else comes of this venture, we can always say we had some laughs while it was being written.

ISBN-10: 1-945393-50-5
ISBN-13: 978-1-945393-50-1

Also Available by Mary Reason Theriot:
The Hunter
The Traveler
Dr. Frankenstein
Above Suspicion
Horror In The Night
Coming Soon:
Echoes On The Bayou
Seven Deadly Sins
A Kiss So Deadly
A Deadly Combination
www.maryreasontheriot.com

Prologue

Almost hidden in a bend of one of the smaller bayous
in southern Louisiana was a small town named Hope.
The residents of Hope had such a *Joie de vivre,* a joy of
living, about them.

This picturesque town came complete with the charm
to match. The bayou looked serene with the weeping
willow trees and cypress trunks, as if right off a
postcard.

Plantations in this area have been used in movies for
several years. With their well-manicured landscaping
and huge antique oak trees complete with the Spanish
moss hanging down, they provided the perfect
backdrop. They depicted an era of time in Louisiana
that seemed to be forgotten.

Several southern antebellum plantations withstood the
sands of time here. Most have been passed down
from generation to generation.

But now, a dark cloud hung over the town. Evil lurked
about, keeping to the shadows, waiting. Somewhere
in the night, a killer planned out his hunt. Only he
knew what sick and twisted tortures he had planned.

Hope was usually a close knit community. Murder,
much less serial killer, were not words spoken here —

until now. No one in this little town would have ever suspected that among the smiling faces lived a sadistic killer.

For you see, while secrets could be buried, some never tend to remain buried forever. They have a way of surfacing when you least expect it.

Chapter 1

Tucked away in a far corner among other parcels of land, a lone slave house, appropriately called The Hideaway, and the old buggy trail winding its way through the property, were all that remained of a once majestic plantation. Over the decades the plantation had crumbled and long been forgotten.

The area remained basically untouched. Some who bought the land used it as pastures for grazing, but most used it for hunting camps. The almost desolate area was teaming with wildlife, making it the perfect hunting ground. The Hideaway had been in The Hunter's family for years. Mother Nature and the elements failed to destroy it.

Crape Myrtle trees lined the driveway to the house. Wisteria grew along the rusty old barbed wire fence. It looked to be such a peaceful place. Sometimes, nothing was ever as it appeared.

The Hunter's parents came here to escape the hustle and bustle of the city. It was a quiet place, a place where no one could hear a scream.

The Hunter would always be grateful his father taught him how to hunt; to stalk prey without being noticed. He could crouch in a spot and sit for hours. Growing up, he hunted to escape his father, escape reality. Many times he dreamed of his dad having a horrible hunting accident. For some reason, he had never built up the courage to actually make that particular dream come true.

The Hideaway overlooked the bayou. The back porch was the perfect place to sit and relax. Several cypress and magnolia trees grew along the bayou, giving it a spectacular ambiance. His mother had poured all her love into the landscaping. She wanted it breathtaking, something her friends would talk about. And since his parents passing, he had continued the upkeep.

A pier with a gazebo at the end reached into the bayou. This is where his mother would sit and read a book while he and his dad fished. This place became her escape from reality.

Not far from the house sat an old cemetery. His mother despised the cemetery. She made sure it blended into the landscape by planting rose bushes around the cemetery plot with magnolia trees framing the back.

He played in the cemetery often as a child. He would hide behind some of the ornate tombstones and scare his mother half to death when she came looking for him. His mother never liked for him to play in there, or outside for that matter. She had forbidden him from getting dirty when he was younger. As he grew older, she learned to fear him more than she ever feared his father. Perhaps she saw into his soul, if he ever even had one.

Chapter 2

When The Hunter discovered that hunting wild animals no longer offered him a challenge, he moved on to a different type of prey. One he could enjoy playing with more.

He lived for the thrill of the hunt. He didn't always have an actual victim picked out. He wanted to find his prey, follow them, and move in for the capture.

The capture of the victim made him feel in control, but it was the kill that made him feel all powerful. He wanted to show these women they were the weaker sex compared to him.

He had his gloves in his pocket ready to go. He preferred the thin ones; it gave him a better grip on his tools, allowed him to feel more. He wanted to feel the blood on his bare hands, but he couldn't risk leaving fingerprints. His body would have to do.

He wore a baseball cap to contain what hair he had. He preferred his military cut since he was too vain to shave his head bald. He just had to be careful because hair follicles could leave DNA if left behind. He had paid for laser hair removal years ago in Springport to remove his body hair. The lady never even asked him why, as if it was a daily occurrence there.

He even purchased booties for his shoes. This would throw them off on any definable shoe prints. Plus, he had shoes in different sizes. Bigger and smaller, never the exact size he actually wore. He would keep them guessing each time he went for a hunt. That was if they even looked for his footprints. He doubted the local police department here knew anything about that.

In the beginning, The Hunter found his prey in Springport and surrounding cities. They consisted mainly of women he found in or around the shelters. Some were just runaways walking the streets, looking for a warm place to stay. He had lured most with the promise of drugs or alcohol.

He preyed on women who would not be missed. After all, he had just started hunting for human prey and must practice before moving closer to home. He brought the victims back to the camp to have his fun with them. He wanted to experiment with various torture techniques. He had to find out which techniques brought the most pain. He soon learned which tortures made the women die too quickly. He wanted to keep them alive for a while and enjoy his new hobby. After all, practice makes perfect.

The torture excited him. His whole body was in tune to the thrills. His skin tingled, and his pulse raced. It was a natural high for him.

He remained extremely calm. No sweaty palms or jittery feelings. This was what he loved to do, what he craved. It was his reason for living.

It could be hard for him to stay in control at times. When their screaming grew louder, he became frenzied in the stabbing. He had to force himself to take his time and make it last. He must show self-control to do this. He needed to practice self-discipline. To learn discipline, he practiced as frequently as possible. The more frenzied he became in the torture, the greater his chance of leaving trace evidence.

Murder could be such an overload to his senses. He found if he just nicked the lung area, they would let out gurgling noises. He enjoyed listening to them gasp for air.

He had a shelf with various assortments of acids in different strengths. He liked to give them manicures in acids. Acid made it extremely difficult to retrieve the fingerprints, if not impossible. He didn't want the bodies identified too quickly. That was part of the game.

The only problem with acid manicures was the timing. If he waited too long, the acid removed the fingertips completely and it did his masterpieces no good to be completely fingerless.

He had considered the addition of pliers to his arsenal of tools. He already had so many to choose from, but could a person ever have too many tools? He may need to start pulling teeth so dental records couldn't be matched. Pouring acid down the throat may help with that too. That would be something else to experiment with.

He learned from experience that some women couldn't take the pain of having all the tortures done at the same time. He didn't want them to pass out from the pain too soon or die too fast. Sometimes it took a while to revive them when they passed out from the pain. Better to take it slow and steady. It is a process he has perfected.

He considered those that he buried his trials. Now he was ready to start showing his artwork.

Chapter 3

Sarah Metzger was a 28 year old high school teacher at St. Anthony's Catholic School. The job was more rewarding here than when she taught in Springport. She thoroughly enjoyed teaching in this small town. She could help the students that needed more attention since the classes were smaller.

Sarah had been so excited when she saw the ad running a year back for the teaching job at St. Anthony's. She needed this change. But it took a bit of explaining to get her parents to understand that she was ready.

She dreamed of finding Mr. Right and settling down. That was one of the main reasons she moved to Hope. She had grown tired of big city life and looking for men in all of the wrong places. She prayed that she would be able to achieve her goal here.

Sarah ran to the grocery store in hopes of being in and out. Her date would be at her house in less than an hour. As usual, she got tied up at work. A student, football player to be more exact, needed extra credit to bring up his grade to be able to play in tonight's football game. Rumors were floating around the school that a scout would be there. Plus the opposing team is one of the school's biggest rivals.

As if she would just give him instant extra credit. She isn't that type of teacher; she believed students needed to earn their grades. Even the coach expressed his annoyance with her about his star football player sitting out of tonight's game.

Now she had to rush to have supper ready in time. The relationship with John Allen was still new and she hoped it led to something more permanent. He was sexy in his own little way, with raven black hair and those deep chocolate eyes that she could get lost in. When he looked at her, she forgot everything else.

A chill ran through her in the checkout line. Looking around, she didn't see anything out of the ordinary. She quickly rushed home to get everything done for her date.

***

Sarah was almost through preparing supper. She doubted John was ready to try her cooking anyhow, so she decided to pick up something. Tonight's menu consisted of store bought rotisserie chicken, with mashed potatoes and gravy and a salad. She did manage to make a cheesecake from scratch. Although she was not a very good cook, she was an excellent baker. And if all went well tonight, she planned on working off the extra calories from the cheesecake.

They say the way to a man's heart is through his stomach. If that's true, her cooking wouldn't get her too far at all. She didn't want this relationship to come to an end over her cooking, or worse, give him food poisoning.

She paused for a moment and gazed out the window, dreaming about all the possibilities that could happen tonight.

* * *

Hiding in the shadows, The Hunter stirred as she glanced in his direction. With the aid of his night vision goggles he could stand far away from her house and still see her.

As he watched her, his cock grew hard at the thought of the things he would do to her. His heart beat faster with anticipation. He patiently waited as she went about her plans, without any notice of him.

The evenings were finally cooling off. It was such a welcome relief from the oppressive summer heat. The air was heavy with the smell of star jasmine that grew around the porch.   It was a perfect night to dine on the screened porch out back.

Sarah took two plates down from the cabinet and began setting the table.

"Tsk, tsk, tsk she is expecting company. That just won't do at all." He had to move fast if he wanted to create a work of art tonight.

He silently made his way to her house, making sure to blend into the surroundings. Carefully, he aimed a rock for the porch light. He didn't want the porch illuminated when he entered the house. An open window in the living room allowed some fresh air inside, and gave him the perfect opportunity to enter undetected. He quickly removed the screen.

* * *

Sarah thought she heard a faint sound come from the living room. Her nerves were strung tight as she anxiously waited for John to arrive. All of a sudden the hair on the back of her neck stood up. A chill rushed over her as goose bumps crawled across her arms.

When Sarah heard the sound again, she stepped into the living room to investigate, just to prove to herself that she was being paranoid.

***

Acting quickly, The Hunter held the chloroform filled rag over her mouth. The exhilaration of the hunt and anticipation of the kill gave him an overwhelming rush. He had to force himself to slow down or he would make a *faux pas*, a mistake. He didn't want to leave any evidence behind.

He moved briskly, with a purpose. She never felt him coming.

***

Sarah awoke dazed. She had a funny taste in her mouth. What happened? Where was she?

She wondered how long she had been out. She tried to clear the fog from her mind and remember what had happened. Her body felt heavy; she had difficulty moving her arms and legs.

She looked down and realized that she was naked, and

strapped to what resembled a dental chair, or maybe an ob/gyn chair. She noticed the room was mirrored floor-to-ceiling.

Her skin began to crawl. Fear rippled through her as she realized someone had kidnapped her. She may not know what he had planned for her, but it couldn't be good. Hopefully John noticed her missing and called the police.

Sarah heard footsteps approaching. As he entered the room, Sarah felt the evil surrounding him. She stared into his black, soulless eyes. He was naked except for the surgical gloves on his hands.

***

The Hunter smirked to himself as he wondered if she would be a challenge or an easy kill. The effects of the chloroform should be wearing off.   He wanted a challenge tonight. He had been perfecting his artistry for quite a while. Now he would show this town what he was capable of; this would be his first masterpiece unveiled.

He set up his recorder to capture her reactions. He wanted to relive the kill over and over. He also needed to learn from any mistakes he may make for next time. He didn't want his work to grow stagnate.

The Hunter laughed at her futile attempts to break free from the restraints. He watched as his laughter caused her to scream, and tears streamed down her face. The more he laughed, the harder she struggled to escape.

"Please, please let me go," she pleaded. "I won't tell anyone. I don't even know where I am. I don't even know who you are. I just want to go home."

"Scream all you want, cher, there is no one to hear you. There is no one to save you."

"Please don't hurt me. Oh God, please don't kill me. I'll do whatever you want. Just let me live. Let me go home."

He chose a beloved torture device to start with. It was a knife sharpener that he ground down into the shape of a long triangle.

The Hunter watched the life fade from her eyes as her blood pooled on the floor. Some of the blood splatter had already started to turn black.

This was the only room in The Hideaway that did not have the original hardwood floors. Before his first hunt, he installed commercial grade vinyl. It was easier to clean the blood from the vinyl than hardwood. He would have preferred concrete flooring, but with the cabin being built off of the ground, that was impossible.

He had installed a drain hole in the middle of the room. It made it easier to hose down the mess before mopping and sanitizing the area.

He looked over the body with a sense of pride. He'd created another a masterpiece, one much better than any of the ones before. This one deserved the privilege of being displayed.

He imagined the horror on their faces when the body was found. No one living here would think of this little town in the same way ever again. They would know what it was like to go to bed afraid. Of course, they would be stunned and confused at first. And, as he unveiled his series, they would be truly scared to go out at night. Nothing like this ever happened around here. People wouldn't know what to think.

The Hunter wanted the perfect place to display his masterpiece. Since the sun wouldn't be up for a few hours, he still had time. He had hoped for her to last longer than she did. Maybe his next victim would be able to take the torture longer.

The night air felt welcoming. He wanted this luxuriously euphoric feeling to last forever. He despised that it had already come to an end.

He had to be careful when he displayed the body. He didn't want to get noticed.

This masterpiece should be a welcoming sight to those coming into town. It was his debut night after all. Before this work of art, he had kept his pastime a secret from everyone. No one knew what cruel fantasies he harbored deep inside the recesses of his mind.

Ripples of pleasure coursed through The Hunter as he remembered his kill. He had denied himself the wicked temptation of taking her, but used the instruments to take the place of his sex organ.

For the first time in a long time, he had a painful erection that had lasted. He was already looking forward to creating his next masterpiece. Maybe with his next kill he would succumb to his carnal temptations. Perhaps the time had come to indulge in some of his sexual fantasies. Condoms would help with containing his semen. With his trial studies, he never had a rush like he did from tonight's masterpiece.

Chapter 4

Sheriff Matthews was on his way home when his cell phone rang. He quickly glanced at the screen and saw it was the dispatcher, he answered.

"Sheriff."

"Sheriff Matthews, we have a man here complaining that his girlfriend is missing. He suspects she has been missing a couple of hours. He is adamant that something happened to her. They are supposed to have supper at her house tonight. When he arrived, the house was open but she was nowhere to be found. Her car is there as well as her purse and cell phone. It's like she just vanished into thin air.

"At first he thought she ran to a neighbor's house to borrow something she may have forgotten. But they haven't seen her either."

"Tell him I'm turning around now. I'll be there in a minute."

***

John Allen saw Sheriff Matthews enter the building and ran up to him.

"Sir, I wouldn't bother you if I didn't think something was wrong. This is not like Sarah. She is a very dependable person. She is a local teacher here at St. Anthony's. We just started dating but she has always been punctual. There's not even a note to say she stepped out. She appeared to be in the middle of preparing supper.”

“Mr. Allen, I will send a patrol car to her house to have a look around. I’m sure there’s nothing to worry about.”

“Sheriff, I’m telling you I have a bad feeling about this. Something just isn’t right.”

“If it will help put your mind at ease, I’ll go over there myself. Just watch, when we get there she will be wondering why you are late.”

“I sure hope I’m wrong about this, but I’m worried about her. She doesn’t live that far from here. On Oak Grove Road.”

“You are obviously shaken up, why don’t you ride with me? We’ll go check it out together.”

***

Sarah lived only a few miles from the sheriff’s office, near the school where she taught. It didn’t take them any time to get there.

“Son, why don’t you stay here?”

“Yes sir. The front door isn’t locked. When I couldn’t find her, I went straight to your office.”

As Sheriff Matthews stepped onto the porch, he noticed the broken porch light. The front door was indeed unlocked, which in all honesty wasn't unusual for around here. Hardly anyone locked their doors, except maybe at bedtime.

Knocking on the door, he called out as he entered the house, "Sarah, its Sheriff Matthews. John asked that I stop by."

Something was definitely off. There were candles lit, supper out and a window in the living room open with the screen missing.

Sheriff Matthews radioed dispatch. "Please send Detectives Sanders and Johnson out here. Make sure Sanders has her crime scene kit to take photos and fingerprints.

"I am at 223 Oak Grove Road. Also, have Deputy Andrews come pick up Mr. Allen. Just have Andrews take him back to the station and get his statement."

"Yes sir."

Chapter 5

As the Guidry family headed out for the day, the gloomy morning greeted them. The clouds from yesterday's storm slowly moved across the sky. The town had been a dust bowl lately, the rain much needed.

As they drove into town, the kids noticed something by the side of the road, propped up against a tree.

"Dad, I think someone is hurt over there. They aren't moving."

He pulled the SUV over to make sure that someone didn't need help. There usually weren't any problems with vagrants around here, but times were tough everywhere.

"You stay here; I'm going to see if they are okay."

At first he thought it was someone who had passed out, but as he moved closer he realized how wrong his assumption was. He couldn't let his wife or kids see this, they would have nightmares forever. It was something he would never forget.

"Hon, you go on to practice. I'm going to call the police and wait for them." He desperately tried to keep his composure.

"I'll have one of the cops drive me over."

As his wife pulled away, he called the police.

"I'm on the edge of town and there's a body over here. I can't say for sure if wild animals got a hold of it or what, but the body is in pretty bad shape."

"We will send a deputy right over."

"I'll be standing on the side of the road waiting."

"Have you gone near the body?" the deputy asked.

"Close enough to know you need to send a coroner and not an ambulance, but that's it."

"Is it someone that you recognize by chance?"

"No. I'm not sure if the person's own mother would recognize them," he answered.

Mon Dieu, who would do this to someone. They must have been really angry.

Chapter 6

Detective Jordan Sanders was the only female the town of Hope had on its force. In actuality, she was the only female on the force for the neighboring towns also.

Her parents desperately wanted a son after already having had five girls. When she came along her dad swore that he would finally have a son. Surprise, it was another daughter. They decided to keep the name Jordan. It seemed to fit her perfectly. Out of all her sisters, she was the only tomboy. She was her dad's shadow. While growing up, he taught her how to shoot a gun as well as a bow and arrow. They would hunt and fish together on his off time. They were like two peas in a pod.

Her dad had been on the police force as well, having only recently retired. He allowed her to ride with him when she was younger. Being a cop was in her blood and no one could talk her out of it, even though her mom tried her hardest.

Being sheriff never interested her dad. He was happy being a deputy. He didn't like all the paperwork that came with being sheriff. Plus, all of the politics the job involved.

Now Jordan, on the other hand, has her sights set high. If only the people in this town would realize that a woman could indeed be sheriff. She will have to prove herself first.

People have told her since she joined the force that she didn't fit the definition of a cop by a long shot. Her height was the same as most men, right at 5'11''. Weighing in at one hundred twenty pounds soaking wet, and her thick, unruly auburn hair, large breasts, blue eyes and a thin physique, she looked more like a model. Thankfully a minimizer bra helped to hide her figure.

Even with her looks, she could hold her own. She had been taking karate since the age of five. By fifteen, she was an experienced black belt. In a small town with not much else to do, she practiced karate religiously.

Chapter 7

Jordan enjoyed her Saturday mornings. It was the only day that she had to herself. Sundays were spent with her family; listening to her mom lecture her on how she needed to settle down and give her some grandkids. Not that her parents didn't have enough grandchildren from Jordan's sisters. And dinner always followed mass, no matter what.

The smell of coffee filled the air. She was trying to decide what to prepare for breakfast when her phone rang.   If the dispatcher was calling, it couldn't be good. Saturdays were usually quiet in this small town.

"Sanders."

"We have a dead on arrival as you are coming into town. The call just came in. Deputy Andrews is on scene. He said to bring your kit, it's bad."

"I'll call Johnson and let him know."

"Thanks. I'll give the sheriff a heads up."

She dreaded calling Johnson, but they needed to work the scene together in case it was more than a simple accidental death. Highly unlikely in this town, but times were changing everywhere. Due to the declining economy, the town had already had more burglaries in the last month than it did all of last year.

She wasn't surprised when Johnson picked up on the first ring.

"Hey Kyle, have you…" she started before he interrupted her.

"I heard the news over the scanner. I woke up Lacy to finish fixing the kiddos pancakes. I'll meet you out there."

With that, he hung up the phone. She quickly went to get dressed before heading to the scene.

As she rushed off, she dropped the top of her car. She may as well get some enjoyment from this now wasted Saturday.

Her one indulgence in life was a '68 Mustang convertible in mint condition. She and her dad restored it together over the years, father/daughter bonding time. She loved to drive the car whenever she could, especially with the top down.

The temperature was in the mid 70's, perfect weather for down here. It had been a long, hot summer and fall was late getting started. Some people prefer Christmas, but she loved fall.

***

Deputy Andrews was taking down notes when she arrived. He was all business this morning. Mornings here do not consist of a body being found on the side of the road.

The body resembled a broken Marionette doll from

this distance. As she approached the crime scene, she realized the horrific torture this person went through. *Pauve ti bête, poor little thing.* She prayed that the torture had been performed postmortem.

But Jordan's gut told her that this sadistic SOB did it while she was still alive and fighting. He wanted her to feel every cut and burn.

The body resembled a female, but it was hard to tell by looking. The breasts had been completely removed. Her body was laid up against a large oak near the road. Whoever did this wanted her body to be found. The body had been posed deliberately, not just dumped here.

Her mind kept going back to the distraught boyfriend and a presumed missing teacher, Sarah Metzger, from last night. As of this morning she still had not been heard from, maybe until now.

One look at the body confirmed that this was not an accident, hunting or otherwise. There's no way wild animals did this to her. No, someone did this on purpose.

There were cops everywhere. This was a new experience for them. She couldn't remember the last murder this town had.   Manslaughter, yes, but an actual homicide didn't occur.

Jordan speculated if this case was an isolated murder or a prelude to something more? Her gut told her they may have a monster lurking here in this town, and he was just getting started.

Chapter 8

Sheriff Matthews planned to spend his Saturday morning relaxing and doing absolutely nothing. Other than maybe catching up on the news. His wife, Mindy, went to the flea market with some of her friends. He had the house to himself and Mindy didn't even leave him a honey-do-list.
When his phone rang, a feeling of dread came over him. Usually his deputies didn't bother him unless it was something important.

"*Bon jour,* good morning, Andrews. What seems to be the problem?"

"Well sir, we received a call about a dead body on the side of the road as you are heading into town, on Highway 24. Detectives Sanders and Johnson are en route now."

"Can you please repeat that? I'm not sure I heard you right."

"Mais non sir, you heard me right."

"I'm on my way."

"Sir, I just want to warn you it's bad. It reminds me of the horror movies I watched as a teenager."

***

It wasn't long before Sheriff Matthews arrived at the crime scene. Detective Johnson was finishing up with the man who called in the body.

Jordan walked over to Sheriff Matthews. "Sheriff, here is what we have so far. A family was on their way to softball practice this morning when one of the kids noticed something by a tree. The father pulled over to see if he could help and received the surprise of a lifetime. I don't think this will be something he soon forgets. Thankfully, the wife and kids stayed in the car. Honestly, I didn't believe it when the call came and it's nothing like I've ever seen before. At first I thought it was a prop from the haunted house for Halloween.

"Deputy Andrews diverted traffic to keep out any onlookers. She hasn't been here long. The coroner is on his way, but I believe this is Sarah Metzger."

"That's what I am afraid of Sanders. I've already talked to the mayor, I'm requesting assistance from the state troopers. Not that I don't trust you, or the rest of the deputies, but the state has a better crime scene unit readily available. Let's keep this under wraps for as long as possible. I know in this town it's hard, but we don't want mass panic about a murder as well." Running his hand through his hair he asked, "What do you know about Sarah Metzger?"

"Not much. She has been teaching here for a year over at St. Anthony's. She was tired of big city life and wanted a place she could find someone special to settle down with. No kids. Never married. Her parents live in Springport.

"She has had a few dates with John Allen. He's local,

works at the mechanic shop. I don't see John doing something like this. Hell, I don't see any of the locals doing anything like this.

"Since Hurricane Katrina, we have had some new people move in but they all seem to be well-rounded decent citizens."

Chapter 9

The need to kill again became overpowering. His latest prey, Sarah, had died way too quick for his liking. Even though she withstood the torture through most of the night, she didn't have the fight in her that he craved, needed. She lasted longer than any of his previous prey, but he wanted a real challenge. One that lasted all night, if not longer. He'd never had a victim to make it a full day.

He considered making a trip to Brighton, Mississippi. There was a mall there and he may have a better selection of prey. Perhaps a young mother, someone that had something to live for. Besides, he had to be careful hunting another local so soon after the last kill.

He preferred to hunt at night, but wanted to take a risk today. Attempting an abduction in broad daylight would be extremely risky. Besides, he couldn't wait until nightfall.

Chapter 10

Marilyn Hennessey was busy shopping and preparing for her daughter's birthday. Carolyn, her soon to be seven year old daughter, insisted on an Arabian themed party thanks to *Aladdin*, which she was currently hooked on.

Hopefully she could find almost everything in one place. She wasn't in the mood to spend her day shopping. She was excited when she found her prayers were answered. She found party decorations and favors on sale as well as costumes since Halloween had just passed. The children would be able to dress up and really get into the party.

If the weather cooperated, everything could be set up outside. It would be cute to have tents with the pillows from the patio furniture thrown onto the ground. Maybe place a rug on the ground as their flying carpet. It would create a true *Aladdin* experience.

Marilyn was busy thinking of party plans and never heard the stranger come up behind her.
Marilyn never felt someone cover her mouth with chloroform and drop her in the back of the van. Her last conscious thought was about arranging games to play outside.

***

On the drive back to The Hideaway, The Hunter thought about the glorious tortures he would use. The anticipation became too much. He wondered how she would handle the pain.

She had to have a child because of the items she bought. Maybe that would give her a reason to fight. Oh yes, maybe indeed!

***

As she came to, Marilyn believed she was in a moving vehicle. It felt like they were traveling down a gravel road. How long had she been out? Where was he taking her?

She thought about her family. Her daughter should be getting out of school soon. Carolyn would be frantic when she didn't pick her up. Hopefully the school would call Stan to let him know she hadn't picked up Carolyn. She prayed that someone would call the police and that she would be saved before anything happened to her.

When she realized that her arms were restrained above her head, she started to make a plan of escape. All of those tv shows she had been watching lately had to be good for something.

When he opened the van doors, she started kicking at him. She feared this may be her only chance at escape.
She managed to get a good kick in and knocked her captor down. She took off running.

Unfortunately for Marilyn, he had a stun gun and was

quicker than her.

"You bitch." Her captor grabbed her and threw her over his shoulder, "You will pay for that."

The electrical current ripped through her body when he struck her with the stun gun. Her last thoughts were of fear as darkness over took her. When she came to she was shackled to some kind of twisted dentist or OB/GYN chair.

Marilyn felt defeated as tears flowed down her cheeks. She wasn't ready to die. She needed to get control of herself; tears wouldn't help her.

She heard footsteps approaching. As the door opened, her captor stepped in naked except for the surgical gloves on his hands.

"Please, please let me live. I want to see my sweet, sweet Carolyn grow up."

"Do as I say and perhaps you will see your Carolyn again." The way he said it, Marilyn knew she wouldn't.

When the torture began, he started off by prying her eyes open. She watched in pure horror as his facial expressions changed right in front of her. Evil consumed him all at once.

The mirrors were everywhere, floor to ceiling. She couldn't help but watch the torture he did to her body. It was psychological torture as well as physical.

Her life would end by the hands of her captor. At any time, this may be her last breath. She would never see her daughter grow up, graduate, get married, or have children. She wished death would take her. She wanted the excruciating pain and suffering to end.

She didn't want to be revived again.

She let out a chilling scream. "Why won't you let me die?"

Smirking at her he replied, "Because we aren't done playing yet."

As her body grew weaker, the man asked, "How does it feel to know you are going to die? And that I control when?"

***

After several hours of her screaming, he couldn't take anymore. The incessant screams had become a distraction rather than a turn on. They seemed to bounce off the walls in the tiny room. He desperately tried to stay in control in an attempt to make the torture last longer.

The duct tape didn't work in silencing her, it had come loose. While super gluing her mouth closed may have worked, he instead stitched her mouth shut for good measure. Oh yes, she had some fight in her. He wasn't ready to let her die. Each time he noticed her slipping into unconsciousness, he would revive her.

The tortures he performed on her body gave him an erection like never before. He'd already ejaculated several times.

This hunt had brought him a lot of thrill and excitement. His control started to slip; but he couldn't force himself to slow down. He became caught up in the moment now that he didn't have to listen to the bitch screaming anymore.

He watched as the light left her eyes. She didn't disappoint him. She managed to last all night and into part of the morning. Not quite twenty-four hours, but more than any other victim.

Tranquility came over him as the life left her body. He was exhausted sexually and mentally. He couldn't dispose of the body until tonight. This masterpiece would be even better than the previous. He couldn't wait to display this one. It had to be placed somewhere grand. Come nightfall he would prepare her for her showing.

Chapter 11

Stan Hennessey's cell phone rang. He was shocked when saw it was Carolyn's principal, Mrs. Gillespie.

"Mr. Hennessy, I'm sorry to bother you, but Marilyn hasn't made it to the school to pick up Carolyn. We haven't been able to reach her."

"I apologize. She must not be paying attention to the time. She planned to shop for Carolyn's birthday party this weekend. I'm on my way."

"See you soon then."

Stan couldn't help but worry. It wasn't like Marilyn to forget to pick up Carolyn. He tried her cell and it just rang so he left a message. She planned to go shopping for the party, but she should have been done hours ago. Marilyn detested shopping, and preferred to get it done as fast as possible. He always considered himself lucky in that regard.

After he picked up Carolyn he drove to their house. Marilyn's car wasn't there. Stan decided to drop Carolyn off at his parents and go look for Marilyn.

"Mom, I'm going to see if Marilyn is still at the mall. This is so unlike her. I left a note at the house letting her know where Carolyn was. If you hear from her, please have her call me."

"Of course, dear. It'll be okay. I'm sure time just got away from her."

With that he went in search of his wife. If he saw her car still in the mall parking lot, he could always have the mall page her.

She was a creature of habit and always parked in the same spot. She had been so excited when he surprised her with her new Toyota Highlander. She always parked it in the back of parking lots to keep it from getting hit by car doors, buggies and such.

Sure enough, he found Marilyn's car still in the parking lot.

Stan noticed what he thought to be Marilyn's purse on the ground and maybe her keys too. Which was odd; it wasn't like her to lose her purse. She kept everything but the kitchen sink in that thing. He looked around for Marilyn, but didn't see her. With a heavy sense of foreboding, Stan called 911.

"This is Stan Hennessey. I'm at the Edgewood Mall. My wife, Marilyn Hennessey, never picked up our daughter from school. Her car is still in the mall parking lot with her purse and keys on the ground. She seems to be nowhere around though."

"Sir, please do not touch anything. I will have a patrol car over as soon as possible," the dispatcher said.

"Okay, mall security just arrived."

"Please ask them not to touch anything either. We also need to see if the mall has video surveillance in the parking lot. That will allow us to track her movements."

Stan quickly turned to the security guards and repeated what the dispatcher said.

"I'm sorry," said the first guard, "but we don't have cameras out this far."

With a shake of his head, Stan quickly told the dispatcher, "Mall security just explained that they do not have cameras in the back part of the parking lot, only the front mall entrances."

"Ok sir, I need you to stay there with the security guards. The patrol car is on its way to you now, so please wait for them to show up."

When the cops arrived, they started asking Stan questions. They still questioned if she simply walked away from her family. However, since her purse and car keys were found lying in the parking lot, they waived the usual 48 hour waiting period.

The officer kept asking, "Are you sure your wife didn't have a boyfriend and they decided to run off together?"

"I know my wife, she wouldn't just walk away. Especially without our daughter. Carolyn meant the world to her. Things were finally looking up for us. Our marriage has the same problems as most marriages, but it was a happy marriage. Besides, if she had run off with another man, she would still take her purse. Something is terribly wrong."

"We need to consider all scenarios Mr. Hennessey. Our best bet will be reaching out to the media for help. We need to get it on the news as soon as possible about your wife going missing. Perhaps someone shopping at the mall today noticed something in the parking lot and didn't realize it was important. An out of place vehicle maybe, someone talking to your wife, anything."

"Anything you need. I just want my wife brought back home alive and well."

"That is our goal also, Mr. Hennessey."

Chapter 12

Jordan was finishing up her daily reports as well as looking over the state troopers' crime scene reports when the ten o'clock nightly news came on. Even though the missing woman resided in Brighton, Mississippi, for some reason it caught her attention. It had to be a coincidence. People went missing all the time. Since their missing person's case had turned out so bad it made her paranoid. It'd been almost a month and no other women had gone missing here and no more mutilated bodies were discovered. So far her fears were unfounded, which she was extremely thankful for.

Perhaps Sheriff Matthews was right and it had been someone passing through town. Still, the state troopers offered their assistance with solving the murder. Besides, they were accustomed to handling murders on almost an everyday basis.

Unfortunately, neither of them had any leads on the killer's identity. She hadn't given up hope that the killer would be caught and neither had the troopers helping to investigate the case.

John Allen still had not been cleared. Although, personally she did not believe he committed the murder. He was too shaken up by Sarah's death, and that wasn't something that could be faked.

Chapter 13

The Hunter awoke from a deep sleep confused. Was the previous night's hunt a dream or was it real?

When he entered his special room, he realized that it was delightfully real. The camera managed to record all of it. She had not disappointed him. This was one truly to savor.

The rain had let up, but it left the air murky. Darkness shadowed the camp. He would most definitely need to move the body tonight. Rigor had begun to set in, and the scent of death was already clinging to her.

He had slept longer than he intended to. He still had to prepare the body for her showing. He cleaned the body thoroughly, removing any evidence. He found that cleaning the body proved to be a little trickier with rigor setting in. He must remember that for the next time, because everything had to be perfect for his masterpiece.

He already knew of the perfect place to display her, the Town Center.

The Saturday market would be setting up in a few hours. The sheriff and his lackeys couldn't keep this one quiet if everyone saw his work. This one was a true masterpiece too; her true beauty showed in his latest artistry talent. She should be seen and not hidden from the public. She resembled a rag doll, but broken and disheveled.

* * *

After disposing of the last body, The Hunter had removed the carpet from the van and burned it. Blood and bodily fluids had proved to be difficult to clean out of carpet. Plus carpet, he realized too late, left fibers on the body. It was best to have a van that he could hose out and thoroughly clean with bleach.

Everything had to be kept sterile. Now that he was displaying his masterpieces, instead of burying them, he needed to be extra careful about trace evidence. He didn't want to get captured.

* * *

Deputy Andrews was doing his early morning patrols when something in the Town Center caught his attention. It looked to be as though someone fell asleep by the flagpole. He retrieved his flashlight and headed toward the flagpole to investigate. As he neared the body, he could tell this one was worse than before.

He quickly called the Sheriff. He hated to be the one to ruin another Saturday.

"Sheriff, I know you don't want to hear this on a Saturday morning but we have another body. It's in the Town Center, right at the flagpole. I plan to call Detective Sanders next."

"Please don't tell me it looks like the same guy."

"Sorry, sir, but it does. It looks like he stitched this one's mouth shut too."

"*Pauve ti bête*. Same amount of torture?"

"This one is even worse than the last. Rigor may have set in before he could move her. She appears to be stiff."

"*Quoi d'autre?*"

"Sir?"

"Just wondering what else could go wrong. I'm on my way. I'll call the state troopers' crime scene unit and have them head on out."

Chapter 14

Jordan knew when the caller ID showed Deputy Andrews' name that it wasn't good.

"We have another body in Town Center. This killer is deranged. Oh heaven almighty, *pauve ti bête*, he sewed her mouth shut. Once again he mutilated the breasts. This is one sick SOB.   Why would someone do this?"

"I honestly have no idea. Does Sheriff know?"

"I called him first. He's on his way and is calling the state troopers."

"I'll stop by and pick up Johnson on the way in."

"Sounds good. I'll see you when you get here."

After hanging up the phone, Jordan put her head in her hand. She couldn't believe that the killer had struck again. It seemed as though her fears were coming true when it came to this man. She shook her head and picked up the phone again, this time to call Johnson.

"Johnson? I just got the call from Andrews'."

"Oui, I just hung up with him. Are you still coming to pick me up?" he asked quickly.

"Yes, I'm leaving right now. Be ready to go in a few." Jordan hung up the phone and headed out the door.

***

When they arrived at the scene, Sheriff Matthews called Jordan over. "Do you recognize the body by chance? I know we didn't have any missing person reports to come in.   The state troopers are sending out the crime scene techs."

"Sheriff, this poor woman's own mother wouldn't recognize her. We need to quarantine off this area. The market vendors will be here shortly and no one needs to see this. We should also put up a tent around the scene until the troopers can get here."

"I'll have the dispatcher call some of the off-duty deputies to help out."

A while later the coroner approached them. "We are getting ready to transport her. I'm putting a rush on the autopsy for you. My initial thoughts are that she passed away sometime early yesterday morning.   Rigor has already set in and she's decomposing.

"He tortured her longer than the last victim; some of the wounds have begun to scab over.

"The mutilation was gruesome. I still can't figure out why someone would want to do that to another human being."

"Thanks doc."

Chapter 15

Sunday morning's paper had a brief article about the missing woman in Brighton, Mississippi. Jordan recalled the news report from Friday night. They had an unidentified Jane Doe and no locals reported missing. Maybe this poor woman was their missing woman.

Jordan called the Sheriff to discuss the possibility with him. "Sir, did you see this morning's paper?"

"I just sat down with it. Why? Please don't tell me our latest murder victim was front page news before we have even identified her."

"No sir. It seems there is a woman over in Brighton, Mississippi that has been missing since Thursday. I hope for her family's sake that our murder victim isn't this Marilyn Hennessey. I plan to call the sheriff there and get some more particulars on the case. Unless, of course, you would rather make the call?"

"This is your case, I'll let you handle it as you see fit. Good thinking though."

"Thank you, sir. Appreciate it."

After talking to the Brighton Sheriff's office, Jordan had more questions than answers. There were a lot of similarities in the women's disappearances. She said a silent prayer that this body didn't belong to their missing woman, but her gut told her it was her.

***

The Brighton sheriff's department requested Marilyn's dental records and a strand of her hair for them to compare.

They drove straight to the coroner's office so that the records could be compared. A positive ID came back quicker than they expected.

"Sheriff, its Sanders. We have confirmation. It is Marilyn Hennessey from Brighton. How did you want to handle this?"

"I'll contact the Brighton Sheriff's Department and see what they want to do about it."

***

Sheriff Matthews agreed to meet Sheriff Harmon, Brighton's sheriff, at their sheriff's department and do the notification collaboratively.

When Mr. Hennessey opened the door, he looked as if he hadn't slept since his wife went missing. Unfortunately, it was about to get a lot worse for him.

By the time they were done with the notification, night had fallen. It had not gone well at all.

He could feel the cold front moving in. The night matched Sheriff Matthews's mood. While driving back to town, he worried the small, once peaceful, town had a serial killer. One like the world had never seen.

This was truly a twisted, sadistic SOB.

***

Sheriff Matthews, the mayor, Johnson, and Sanders had met with the state troopers later that evening. Everyone agreed that the state troopers should set up a mobile command center in town for the time being. Sheriff Matthews invited the FBI in since Marilyn Hennessey had been transported across state lines.

Sheriff Matthews knew that some local law enforcement agencies refused to ask the FBI for help. However, he had no qualms about asking for help with regards to this case. He also knew none of his deputies would give them any grief. Everyone wanted this killer caught.

The FBI planned to run the particulars through VICAP to see if any other hits came up in another state. They seemed doubtful that this guy woke up one day and decided to start killing, especially with the murders as gruesome as they were.

Chapter 16

Sheriff Matthews stepped in front of the reporters. The public needed to be informed of the recent murders, but he detested not having answers to their questions.

The mayor and district attorney had agreed with him that a press conference was necessary, even though they didn't have answers to any questions they may ask. They wanted to avoid panicking the town, but make them aware of the possible dangers.

"I'm just going to make a general statement to the public, nothing more. No questions will be answered.

"Yes, another body has been found. It is believed to be another homicide. This makes two in the last month. We are asking all women in the viewing area to please be careful at this time. When out, be aware of your surroundings. When home, lock your windows and doors."

The sheriff was quickly interrupted with all the questions being thrown at him by the reporters.

"Do you have any suspects?"

"Do you think it could be a copycat?"

"Do you have any clues?"

"Is it true the FBI has been called in? What about the state troopers?"

"I'm sorry, but no questions will be answered at this time. We are still investigating," he stated firmly.

Chapter 17

Andrea Smith was a 26 year old that had spent all her life in Hope, Louisiana. She loved it here and couldn't imagine living anywhere else. She even enjoyed working at the post office. She had a chance to meet with people every day and make small talk.

It was a lovely afternoon when she made it home from work. She decided a run down the road would be a perfect way to wind down after a stressful day. The post office was busier than usual and the Christmas season was just gearing up.

If work wasn't stressful enough, Thanksgiving was a week away and it was her turn to host dinner. Since her mother's passing, her dad preferred to go to his children's houses instead of hosting the holidays at the house they grew up in.

She and her brother had been desperately trying to convince him to sell. The house was too much for him and it held too many memories there. He preferred to live in the past and didn't want to move on. Andrea loved her mom dearly, but even she would want her husband to move on with his life.

She went over the Thanksgiving menu one more time while getting ready for her run. It was a given that they had to have turkey and Mama's oyster dressing. This year Andrea considered being adventurous and adding something new to the traditional Thanksgiving menu.

Andrea dressed for her run and headed out. She had her iPod and earphones on and took off at a slow, leisurely pace with no hurry.

She was being paranoid, but swore she was being watched. Looking back, she didn't notice anything out of the ordinary.

Chapter 18

"It is time for my next masterpiece," The Hunter said to himself.

He desperately needed to hunt. Every inch of his body pleaded with him to go find his prey. He was too anxious, and was getting agitated. He could no longer just close his eyes and relive the last kill, and watching the DVD's did not help bring back the excitement.

He couldn't wait any longer. The need propelled him. It rushed through his veins.

The Hunter first noticed Andrea at the post office. He wanted her desperately for one of his masterpieces. He followed her home one day to see if she had family and started his plan.

Yes, she would be a perfect subject; athletic and young. She may be just the challenge he was looking for. She might last twenty four hours. That was his goal. To prolong death for her a little longer than his previous prey.

As he drove to Andrea's house, he noticed her running on the side of the road. Perfect, it was a good thing he'd brought his tranquilizer gun. With one sure shot, he watched as she started to fall to the ground.

He quickly loaded her into the van. Checking once more, he was positive no one saw a thing.

She was a little heavier than she looked. Yes, she may

do very well for his next project. This one should be a fighter.

Andrea should be out for a while. He gave her a little extra sedative to make sure she remained unconscious while he prepared her.

***

While sedated, he started to glue and sew her lips shut. But he needed her awake to pry her eyes open. It was imperative that she saw what he did to her. That was part of the thrill, to torture them psychologically as well.

He slapped her face to start waking her up. The drug was wearing off, but not fast enough. The anticipation had become overwhelming and he couldn't hold off any longer.

***

Andrea felt a stinging sensation as if someone were slapping her face. She was still very groggy and for some reason she couldn't move. Something was wrong with her mouth; it hurt like hell and she couldn't open it.

Cold dread washed across her. She had heard rumors about a body being found a couple of weeks ago in the town center. It had to be rumors, nothing like that ever happened here.

"I have to fix your eyes first. I want you to see

everything I'm doing. I am sorry about your mouth, but I can't take the screaming after a while, you understand. It can be distracting."

She learned that if she tried not to moan it pissed him off. The calmer she became, the worse the torture. She could barely endure it.

However, she refused to give him the satisfaction of knowing how much pain he caused her.

As she began to zone out again, she heard his voice. "Andrea, Andrea? Stay with me. I'm so glad I chose you as my next masterpiece, but you don't want to disappoint me. You must stay conscious. It won't do either of us any good if you aren't awake during the preparation."

Masterpiece? Masterpiece? What was he talking about?

The super glue severely burned her eyes. That voice, it sounded familiar. She tried to make out the figure, he looked familiar. And then it clicked, he was always in the post office. It couldn't be him, though, he was a computer geek not a killer!

He moved even closer, talking to her softly. "You will be my greatest work yet Andrea.   You will be magnificent."

Andrea tried to jerk loose from the restraints, but was strapped down too tight. *Heaven help me.* She felt the burning. *What was he doing? Was he burning her with a cigarette?*

Then she felt a knife cut into her flesh. It felt like he was cutting her everywhere.

She was ready to beg for a quick death. She didn't want to die, but the pain was excruciating. How long had he been torturing her? She went in and out of consciousness. Just when she thought he would allow her to die, he revived her and began again.

She prayed for death now. A sweet, sweet release from this pain. She heard her mother's voice telling her to stop fighting and come join her. Could it be? Was that really her mother talking to her or was she hallucinating from the pain? She no longer wanted to fight death. Andrea forced her body to relax and followed the sound of her mother's voice into the light.

***

The Hunter saw the life leave her body. He was thoroughly satisfied with his work. He wouldn't be able to revive her again. He finally broke her resolve. She lasted longer than he would've ever imagined. It took almost 48 hours for Andrea to succumb to the torture he put her through.

He was beginning to get frustrated. He had displayed two masterpieces already and still none of his work was featured in the newspaper. He wanted recognition. He would make sure this current masterpiece was noticed tomorrow. Andrea would show up for work in the morning, and she wouldn't be late.

Chapter 19

The postal manager knew it wasn't like Andrea to miss work. When she didn't show up on Saturday and he hadn't heard from her to say she was sick, he started to become worried.

He decided to stop by her house when she didn't answer her phone. There was no answer at her door and her car was in the little garage. He called her brother, perhaps he knew something.

***

When Thomas Smith arrived at his sister's house late Saturday, he noticed right away something was off. Her car was in the garage and her keys were on the hook next to the door. A steak sat on the counter waiting to be cooked, next to a bottle of wine. She appeared to be in the middle of preparing supper, but where was she?

He tried to call her cell phone, but it just rang.

Thomas immediately called the sheriff's department.

"Hope Sheriff's Department, what is your emergency?"

"This is Tom Smith. I'm at my sister Andrea's house on Russo Road. Something isn't quite right here. She's nowhere to be found and it looks like last night's dinner is still on the counter unprepared. She also didn't show up for work this morning."

"Mr. Smith, I'm going to send two detectives out there as well as a patrol car. Please don't touch anything."

***

The dispatcher sent Deputy Andrews to check things out. "I'm calling Detectives Sanders and Johnson as well. You may want to touch base with them."

The dispatcher called Detective Sanders next. "We have another missing person. Andrea Smith from over at the post office didn't show up for work this morning and she's not at home either. Deputy Andrews is heading out there now."

"If it is our guy, he didn't wait a month in between abductions this time. I'll call Johnson if you will call the sheriff. See if he can get the state troopers' crime scene techs headed over there as well."

The dispatcher quickly called the sheriff. "Sheriff, we have another missing person. I already spoke with Detective Sanders and she asked to see if you could get the troopers out to Andrea Smith's house now."

"I'll call them right now. Tell Sanders to wait to touch anything until I get there. I'm heading out now," the sheriff quickly replied.

The dispatcher called Sanders right back. "Sheriff Matthews said he will be out there as soon as possible. The crime scene techs are on their way out and should be there shortly."

Chapter 20

Displaying Andrea's body directly in front of the post office doors was a risky move. People were constantly in and out of the post office, no matter what the time. The Hunter waited until the road was quiet and moved quickly in posing Andrea for work.

As with the other bodies, he didn't bother dressing her. Art was beautiful naked. Yes, this was a true masterpiece. He was creating a very unique series indeed.

***

The post master wanted to arrive at work early this morning. Andrea still had not been heard from since she left work Friday. There was mail to be separated and delivered as well as the usual hustle and bustle of a Monday morning.

When he drove up he noticed something by the front door. It almost looked like someone sitting there, possibly sleeping. He honked his horn to wake the person up. He wasn't in the mood to deal with some drunk or strung out druggie.

If he made enough noise, maybe they would wake up and move along. Nothing happened when he honked his horn though. Looking closer, the pose reminded him of a rag doll sitting there. He made sure to keep his cell phone ready as he exited his car and moved closer to the figure.

He stood there frozen in horror. He couldn't believe his eyes.

The shape of the body almost reminded him of Andrea, but what he was looking at looked like something horror films were made of. He didn't remember calling the police or hearing the sirens. He just remembered sitting in the sheriff's office. He wasn't sure how he got here.

Chapter 21

Jordan saw Sheriff Matthews pull up. "You might want to chew on this."

He looked at her with confusion as she handed him a piece of spearmint gum. "It's bad, sir. I didn't have any vapor rub."

Johnson was already giving orders to the deputies. They set up a tent around her body to keep anyone from seeing her. The coroner had informed Jordan that it would be a while before he could get there.

Johnson looked like he would rather be anywhere but here. She hated to say it, but she felt the same way. This gruesome murder scene was one of the worst she had seen. It was Andrea, or what the killer had left of her.

Sheriff Matthews walked over to where the body was. As he did, Jordan saw his jaw clench.

The similarities were undeniable. There was no doubt in Jordan's mind that Hope had a serial killer.

After the last murder, the media were crawling all over this town. They were worse than buzzards fighting over road kill. They were all trying to get video of the latest crime scene. Sheriff Matthews had instructed everyone on the force not to answer any questions. They needed to let either the State Troopers or FBI handle all the public relations. It was hard enough keeping the locals from being scared out of their minds, without also having to worry with the news crew asking questions.

By the time the coroner arrived, the state troopers' crime scene unit had just finished processing the body.

Jordan noticed the coroner approaching her. "I suspect she has only been dead a few hours. He tortured her for quite some time. I would say for almost two days. I won't know until we do the autopsy, but that is my preliminary findings at this time."

"Thanks Doc. I had figured as much. It seems like just yesterday we found Marilyn Hennessey's body. He's decreasing his time between kills."

The coroner looked stricken. "It's time for him to be caught."

***

Sheriff Matthews walked up to the detectives while they were talking. He looked down at the poor body and made the sign of the cross.

"*Pauve ti bête*, what she must have endured before her death."

Sheriff Matthews felt a headache coming on and rubbed the back of his neck. While the coroner was working on removing the body, the crime scene techs were still processing the rest of the scene. They also had a photographer and videographer capture the scene on film, thanks to the FBI.

Thankfully he had not had breakfast. He would not have been able to keep it down.

He felt completely overwhelmed. This little town didn't get murders such as this. This killer had to be caught and the evil he left in his wake banished from the town.

Sheriff Matthews couldn't help but think aloud. "He is getting more sadistic. He tortured the victims longer, *pauve ti bêtes.*"

Detective Johnson expressed his thoughts on the matter as well. "This is the second local girl murdered and the third to be murdered by the demon. He has developed a signature, prying the eyes open, the mutilations of the breasts and now gluing the mouth shut."

Jordan looked over at Sheriff Matthews. "He's getting riskier with both the abductions and body drops. The last two bodies were possibly abducted during the day. We know for certain that Marilyn Hennessy was and Andrea was abducted while on a run."

Detective Johnson added, "It is a flagrant move to leave the body at the post office's front door. How much cockier can this guy get?" Slamming his fist down on the desk, he asked, "How many more bodies will be left around town before we can nab him? I pray to God that there won't be any more. The SOB has to make a *faux pas* soon."

***

The coroner called later that afternoon. "We may have a break. We found a trace amount of semen on her leg. We are running it through CODIS to see if we get a hit. If there are no hits, we will at least have DNA for when this bastard is caught."

"Thanks doc. Keep me posted," Johnson replied

Detective Johnson headed towards Jordan's desk. "The coroner called. We may have gotten lucky. A trace amount of semen was found on the body."

He went on to inform her, "Sheriff Matthews is having another press conference this afternoon warning women to be vigilant."

Chapter 22

The Hunter smiled. They did not include a photograph of his masterpiece, but it was the front-page story.

He had to be careful hunting too many locals all at once. No reason to get careless now. He also needed to let the story cool down before he killed again.

Chapter 23

News of the recent murder spread like wildfire around town. As Sheriff Matthews entered the department, he noticed Andrea's brother, Thomas Smith, waiting for him.

"Do you have anything new? Have you found her?"

"We are still looking for her." Until Sheriff Matthews had definite confirmation from the coroner, he didn't want to upset the man. The body was in too bad of shape for visual confirmation but with it being left at the post office, Sheriff Matthews believed it was Andrea.

"What about the body that was found? You don't think it's her do you?"

"I'm praying for you and your family that it isn't. But, we have requested dental records for comparison."

"Oh God, it can't be. It just can't be." His eyes were bloodshot and his pallor ashen. There was a quiver in his voice when he talked. "I just don't know how dad will handle the news if it is her."

Chapter 24

After the discovery of the second body, Jordan began studying up on serial killers a little more. Over the years, she had taken a few courses the State and FBI offered, but they merely touched on the subject. Now that they may actually have a serial killer here, she wanted to have as much information as possible on this particular matter.

The evidence and autopsy reports were waiting on her desk the following morning. She poured herself a cup of coffee and sat down.

"Johnson, the reports are here. Did you want to read over them together?"

"Yeah, why don't we all meet in the conference room? I'm sure Sheriff Matthews and the DA will also want to hear what they have to say."

"Works for me," replied Jordan

It was a gorgeous November morning. The sun made its way through the blinds in the room. The splendor of the day did nothing for anyone's spirits in the Sheriff's Office.

Seeing Sheriff Matthews attempting to rub the sleep from his eyes, Jordan passed café au lait around to everyone at the table. "I take it you didn't sleep last night, sir?"

"I haven't slept since the first murder."

There wasn't much to the reports. They read just like the previous two victims. Minimum forensic evidence. No hits in CODIS on the DNA retrieved from the semen. He brutally tortured her for approximately 48 hours. What kind of monster would do this? A normal human being did not commit such atrocities, this person was pure evil.

Sheriff Matthews looked over the group. "There have been three bodies to date. So far the murders were incomprehensible. Does anyone have a clue as to who our UNSUB is?"

Jordan looked around at everyone. "The torture these women sustain is heinous. They would surely scream out in pain. He has to have a discreet place to torture and kill them. In a neighborhood where the houses are close together someone would hear the screaming. Unless that is why he glues the mouth shut. Besides, it would be difficult to sneak a body in and out of a house in a neighborhood. There is always a nosy neighbor."

Johnson chimed in, "This demon has his own brand of cruelty. We need to examine what drives a person to commit this type of crime. The better we understand him, the better our chance is to catch him."

Sheriff Matthews let his feelings known. "I fear the FBI may be withholding information. I'm not saying they are, but so far they are not being very forthcoming with anything that they have found. Three bodies and no clues. How is this possible? Forensics is supposed to be their strong suit.

"The killer does not have a victim type or age preference. At this point any little detail could crack this investigation wide open."

They set up a special board in the conference room with all the women's pictures on it. It was dubbed "The Murder Board". No one liked the name, but that's what it was, a descriptive list of the murders and what evidence they had to date on each murder.

Underneath each picture was the date the victim went missing and the date the body was found. Sheriff Matthews managed to obtain a picture of each victim pre-murder for the board. Regrettably, there wasn't much listed under each photo as far as evidence or information.

They couldn't help but stare at the blasted thing. "The guy is torturing, sexually assaulting and mutilating these women. We have no idea as to his identity. There is little to no evidence to go on. How the hell is that possible?" the sheriff asked.

"Maybe we should ask the public for their help. We could drop a little more information to the reporters. Someone had to have seen something. Possibly someone out hunting or fishing late at night when there is usually no one out, anything. We don't want to encourage a copycat killer or false confessions, but we aren't getting anywhere waiting."

The DA spoke up, "That's an excellent idea. As much

as I hate having a press conference to ask for help, it may be our best option right now. We will put our cards on the table and hopefully someone will know something. Maybe someone did notice something that they don't know is important to the case. We will still have control of the information, and we don't release any vital information."

"Like you suggest, maybe report any suspicious activity during odd hours of the night or early morning.   Possibly release the white utility van information."

Sheriff Matthews spoke up. "I'll run it by the mayor and the FBI, let them get out another press release for us. Good work Sanders, very good thinking. I wouldn't release the information about the white van just yet though. We don't want him to ditch it. That might be our only way to capture him. The deputies are already looking for a white van. Hopefully we can at least get a license plate number and run it, possibly resulting with a suspect."

Murder Board

Victim

Sarah Metzger
Date Missing (DM) – October 2
Date of Death (DOD) – October 3
Carpet fibers from possible Ford van

Marilyn Hennessey
DM – November 3
DOD – November 5
No trace evidence found on/near body

Andrea Smith
DM – November 20
DOD – November 23
Trace amount of semen found on the body

Location

Unknown
Secluded
Isolated
Possible hunting camp?

Unsub

Mid 30's
Possibly drives Ford van, possibly white in color
Caucasian
6 feet, plus
Well-built
In shape

Financially well off
Sexual dysfunction

Personality

Cunning
Superiority complex

Method of Killing

Torture
Rape/sexual assault: pre and post mortem
Breast mutilation
Cleaning body after death

Chapter 25

Sheriff Matthews stepped in front of the reporters. "Thank you all for coming. As I am sure most of you are aware, there have been three murders.

"The State Troopers and FBI have teamed up with us to catch this killer. Rest assured that we are doing everything in our power to make that happen.

"We are also asking for your help. If anyone has seen anything suspicious, we ask that you call the Sheriff's Department. No matter how small it may seem, it can take one small tip to crack the case wide open for us.

"We continue to ask all women in the viewing area to please be careful at this time. Avoid going out by yourself as much as possible."

"Sheriff, are you saying that you do not have any suspects?"

"At this time there are no suspects. That is why we are reaching out to the public," the sheriff answered.

Chapter 26

The Hunter walked through the woods that ran along the back of the camp. He enjoyed the solitude, playing out his next hunt. The woods were his solace growing up. These woods knew all his deep, dark secrets. This was where he dreamed of a different life for himself.

This was where he learned to be silent, watchful. The night had its own special song, with each of the creatures bringing their own special sounds to it.

He walked over to the burn barrel he had made. He placed the surgical gloves and clothes in it. It was better to burn everything and start fresh rather than to wash. No need to chance something being left behind. Nowadays they could find evidence in drain pipes.

He had listened to his dad intently on trace evidence growing up. His dad always talked about how someone was caught because they were too stupid or too lazy to get rid of the clothes or evidence linking them to the crime.

Chapter 27

Nothing compared to living in a small town. Sheriff Matthews preferred it to living in a big city. True everyone tended to know your business, but there was a closeness that a larger city just couldn't compete with.

Hope had always been a peaceful, close-knit community. The population was just under 2800. Hope was so small it didn't have a stop light. Everybody here knew one another, or at least knew of the person. If you didn't know their name, you recognized their face. Going to the grocery store was considered an outing and church was the social event of the week. Whereas most towns in Louisiana were predominately Catholic, this town seemed to be Methodist.

The town had been built along a bayou. At one time it had been a major producer of sugar cane and being built on the bayou was a means of survival.

Great strides had been taken to keep downtown a reminder of the past. For years Hope consisted of mom and pop run businesses. Now a Subway and McDonalds had come to town and rumor has it a Sonic was talking about opening up. The mom and pop businesses made it hard for the fast food restaurants though.

People in Hope believed in supporting their local businesses. Even the grocery store was family owned.

Sheriff Matthews believed he was letting the town

down. It was his job to serve and protect this town and he wasn't living up to his job description. The Sheriff's office was never a dull place to work before the killings, but it was mainly petty crimes; usually teenagers up to mischief.

The murders committed by this killer were too heinous for words. The town seemed to be debilitated by fear.

The town's name of Hope seemed to fit the needs of the town perfectly right now. They all needed to pray and hope that this maniac was captured.

Chapter 28

With the summers being too hot, fall was the perfect season for a carnival in south Louisiana. The hurricane season was officially over first part of November, so that threat was also gone. The town council and mayor had taken everything under consideration when planning out the carnival. Everything, except for a damn serial killer.

The fall carnival had been in the making for a year. A gumbo cook-off, games, rides, vendors, you name it, had been planned for it. With all the vendors and carnival rides planned there was no way the Mayor or town council wanted to cancel. Sheriff Matthews even planned on having extra security. The FBI and State Troopers already offered to provide extra manpower as well. The town desperately needed this to get its mind off of its current situation.

Years ago a factory had started building a plant near the edge of town. When the economy started its downward spiral, the factory went belly up before completion. All that had been built was a steel shell of a building that had been an eyesore.

The Mayor and town council called a special meeting and decided to purchase it last year. They later turned it into a fairground. A roof had been put on the frame, but the exterior walls remained open. Just the steel beams remained exposed.

The Mayor was hoping the carnival would help bring more attention to the local plantations that offered tours. Then you also had the bed and breakfast plantations. The plantation owners all purchased booths for advertisement hoping to increase business. Some planned to offer free coupons for tours and the local bed and breakfast inns were serving samples of their delicious foods.

Of course, this had all been planned before Hope became famous for its serial killer. Now the mayor and the town council feared that this killer would dissuade tourists, and locals for that matter, from venturing out to the carnival.

Chapter 29

As nightfall settled across the campus, the rain that had hung heavily over the area all day finally decided to break free. And Whitney Guillory had forgotten her umbrella. With the dropping temperature she swore that she could see her breath in front of her.

The gaslights cast a watery blue light along the sidewalk and streets.

Whitney knew she shouldn't have stayed at the library so late, but her thesis was due. She couldn't afford to lose her scholarship. She had dreamed of being a doctor since she was ten. Her parents could not afford to send her to college so she depended on that scholarship.

She quickly headed to her rented apartment right off campus. She froze; she swore she heard footsteps behind her. When she looked back, she didn't see anyone.

Suddenly, she heard the noise again. Her heart was racing. Looking back once more, she didn't see anyone in the shadows. She was just being paranoid. She had always been afraid of the dark.

"Is anyone there?" Her imagination must be in overdrive tonight, that's all. She decided to pick up her pace. It was time to get home.

***

Whitney slowly opened her eyes and saw complete darkness surrounded her. A blanket covered her. She was in the bed of a pickup truck with her arms shackled above her. No, wait, that's not right. It had to be a van. There was no one around to help her. Why hadn't she paid more attention to the time?

Panic began to set in. Now was not the time to be scared out of her mind. She needed to keep her wits about her and think. She had to escape. She tried to free her arms from the restraints, but they were too tight.

She suddenly felt a quick jolt, and then darkness once again.

***

Her head lolled back and forth as she slowly woke up. Her mind felt funny, as if she were hung over. She couldn't put all the pieces together. What had happened?

Fear crept up her body as reality set in. She saw her reflection in the mirrors. Her body was restrained in an upright position, almost spread eagle. Her wrists were bound and chained to the ceiling. Her ankles were secured tightly to the floor. She tried to jerk as hard as she could, but there was almost no slack in the chains. Further investigation revealed that the chains were attached to a pulley system, but at this time they appeared to be locked in place.

To make matters worse, she was naked. She heard

footsteps approaching fast. As he entered the room, she cringed at the sight of the naked man.

***

He took in the sight of his prey one more time before he began. Her ample breasts had a rose tattoo almost hidden in the cleavage of one breast. This would be the first tattoo in his collection. He would have to be careful when removing the breasts and tattoo. He didn't want to mar it.

His body craved the sexual release. He throbbed intensely now.

This one's skin was smooth as silk. He bent down to taste her tears. The salty taste overpowered him for a moment. Her breasts were perfectly tanned; no lines marked her beautiful body. She obviously took great pride in her appearance.

These breasts would make a nice addition to his collection. He bit down hard on one nipple and watched her eyes dilate in fear. He let out an ominous laugh.

She died too quickly. The memories of the kill were already dissipating too fast.

The thunderstorm came in hard and fast. It was pitch black outside. Thunder shook the cabin. The rain came down in sheets. With all the noise from the storm, he could put the body in the boat and use the trolling motor without being heard. He would sneak into the town square from the bayou to pose his newest masterpiece. The rain would also help wash away any trace evidence he may have missed.

The carnival would be the perfect place to display the body. He would remind the town that there was no relaxing, no enjoyment, while he was hunting. They shouldn't let their guards down; he could strike at any time.

He decided to show his creation at the Tunnel of Terror ride. He didn't want the body discovered right away giving the sheriff time to close things down.

***

The carnival manager wanted to give the grounds a once over to confirm that there were no glitches. He needed to make sure last night's thunderstorm didn't do any damage. At least the rain had passed and it looked as if the weather would be nice.

This was the carnival's first time here and he wanted to please the town and its mayor. With so many traveling carnivals coming into play, they don't need to lose any customers.

He also needed to make sure no electrical cords were in any water puddles. He doubled checked to make sure they remained hidden under the matting when something by the Tunnel of Terror ride caught his attention. It looked as if someone had left a carcass of some kind by the ride.

He needed to dispose of it and clean the area before people started arriving. He sure didn't need problems right off the bat.

As he moved closer, he thought the thing almost looked human, almost. It seemed to resemble a life sized Raggedy Ann doll. Once he got there he almost passed out.

He immediately called 911. He was barely audible to the dispatcher, "This is the carnival manager. There is a dead body over here!" Stuttering he added, "I, I, I'm not sure if whoever did this is still lurking about."

The dispatcher had trouble making out what he was saying. "Sir, please calm down. I'm going to get Sheriff Matthews out there as quick as I can.

"Would you please stay on the line with me until the deputy or sheriff arrives? I'm dispatching them right now. Just hold on please."

***

Over the radio, the dispatcher contacted Deputy Andrews, "Dwayne, sounds like we may have a dead body over at the carnival. Would you please get over there?   I'm calling Sheriff Matthews right now."

"Sheriff Matthews we have another possible dead body over at the carnival. Deputy Andrews is on his way over. I still have to call Detectives Sanders and Johnson."

"That's all we need today. I'm on my way. I'll call the crime scene techs and FBI to head out there. I want everyone to go in silent. Let's try to keep this low key right now. Maybe we can still save this day."

***

Sheriff Matthews had the crime scene team and FBI meet him out there. "Damn, in four hours the carnival is supposed to open," he said to no one in particular.

He hated to give this killer the pleasure of knowing he closed down something the town had been waiting for in great anticipation.

It was all the kids seemed to talk about this week. They couldn't wait for the carnival rides.

As much as he despised rushing a crime scene, maybe it would be in the best interest of the town to open the carnival. If they could keep this under wraps, with no leaks what so ever.

The mayor and DA agreed to meet there as well. "So, while we are waiting for the coroner let's discuss this. Can we wrap this up as quickly as possible without sacrificing any evidence? I think we should try to save this day if we can."

The mayor and DA agreed that they should try to salvage this day. Even the carnival manager was in agreement. "None of my workers know about this. We should be able to keep the murder under tight wraps on our part. We can quarantine this ride, and area, off just to be safe. Not only would we lose money if the carnival closed, but it would hurt our reputation tremendously. Who wants to book a carnival company where a homicide took place?"

The FBI and crime scene team went into overdrive collecting any evidence that they could find. Unfortunately, it was just like all the previous scenes, nothing substantial. This perp made sure he was careful not to leave any forensic trace evidence behind.

Chapter 30

The killings were monstrous. What did these women have in common besides being murdered in this horrendous fashion?

So little forensic evidence had been left behind. Jordan had more questions racing through her mind rather than answers. They had to stop this sick bastard and fast.

A storm front was moving in fast; the sky was getting dark and gloomy, and the wind began to pick up. At least the carnival was able to take place and nothing had leaked out about the recent murder.

This case was getting to her. Who would kill these women in such a manner? How many bodies would turn up before he was caught? The town was already starting to panic. People now locked their doors. They all looked at their neighbor a little differently now, not sure who to trust.

There were so few clues. She feared that these crimes would remain unsolved. Missing women cases in neighboring areas found their way into the office. On top of everything else, the last body reeked of bleach. With the loss of control he showed recently in the mutilation of the bodies, he began using the bleach to cover any evidence he missed.

This serial killer had his own special calling card. Eyes pried open and the mouth glued then sewn shut. Even the FBI hadn't found any murders like this anywhere else. It appeared they had a homegrown predator here. One that even the FBI had never seen before.

Detective Johnson came back to his desk. "Damn it to hell Jordan, something has to break soon. This creature has to be stopped and stopped soon!"

"I agree. Sheriff just informed me he wants us in his office as soon as the FBI profiler calls. He also plans to ask how much longer it will be before he can get here. I hate to say it, but we need as much help as we can get."

By that afternoon, they continued to wait on the FBI profiler's call. He was working on another case in another state. Montana, she believed. He promised he would call.

***

FBI Agent Alex Hamilton called the sheriff later that afternoon. "Agent Hamilton, I'm glad you called. Can you hold on for a moment while I get my team together?"

"No problem."

"Sanders, Johnson, I got the profiler on the line. Let's move it."

"Agent Hamilton, sorry to keep you waiting. We are all here."

"You've got yourself a problem, Sheriff Matthews. This

guy is escalating faster than most. Serial killers can usually go months in between kills. They start off slow before they feel the need to hunt again. This unsub is a predator. We have to wonder if he stalks his victims or abducts them on impulse.

"As time goes on, the reliving isn't enough and the time shortens between kills.

"I suspect that he has been killing for a while. He is starting to escalate, possibly even starting to devolve. When that happens, the body count will continue to increase before he messes up and is caught.

"He's been taking incredible risks with disposing of the bodies; taking time to pose them. This means he is familiar with the town in some way.

"If you ask me, he is damn cocky. He also wants to taunt you. He wants you to know he's here, in your town. He feels smarter than you. He may be craving publicity and it has been denied to him. Or at least he's not getting the acknowledgement he craves.

"The kill excites him. I know he just started to show signs of sexual contact so be prepared for more of an escalation. He's probably in his 30's and financially secure. Look for someone who has a history of violence or cruelty to animals."

Sheriff Matthews expressed his frustration. "*Masis sa c'est fou.* This is crazy. Between three different law enforcement agencies, someone should be able to find some piece of evidence pointing to a suspect. He's making us all look like fools, an embarrassment to our profession."

"What else do you want us to do Sheriff? We have gone over everything with a fine tooth comb. None of us knows how he is sneaking right past us to dispose of the bodies," a frustrated Deputy Andrews exclaimed.

Sheriff professed, "We have to do something; the whole town is spooked. They have a hard time believing that someone from here is a killer. Handgun sales are going through the roof. Before we know it, there will be an accident. People will eventually start shooting at shadows, anything that goes bump in the night."

He thought about Agent Hamilton's statement, "Cruelty to animals. Hell, that's half the town if you consider the hunters that do it for sport and not for food. It could be almost any male that lives around here."

Agent Hamilton went on to add, "The killer is most probably a sexual sadist. He is unable to climax without inflicting pain or killing. These are the most dangerous of serial killers. They are usually very intelligent yet cunning. They don't look like a maniac, they keep up their appearances. Some can be charming and outgoing. However, some can be shy. He will look like the guy next door. When you find out who he is, you will be completely shocked because he was never on your radar.

"They have no conscience, don't show remorse or

feel guilt for the killings. They fantasize about the pain and torture they want to inflict. They have a plan already. Some stalk a victim for a period of time. This helps them to be prepared and not leave forensic evidence. It makes them harder to catch."

Detective Sanders thought aloud, "He won't stop unless we stop him is what you are saying?"

"That is correct. Thankfully, these sadistic killers are usually rare. Unfortunately, most times, you have to wait until they make a mistake. Or you get really lucky.

"The killer mutilated these poor girls in a horrendous fashion. He was brazen enough to display their bodies in public. He has been daring you to catch him. With each kill and display of the body, he is rubbing it in your face that you haven't caught him. Hell, you weren't even aware that he was killing until he started displaying the bodies. Look at what he is doing. Each murder has become more sadistic with more sexual torture.

"When a killer starts to get careless, he gets more dangerous. More bodies will begin to pile up and faster."

"I agree the killer is escalating," Sheriff added, "The body count is rising fast. He has no timeline for when he kills. I realize that you are busy with this case in Montana, but when can you make an appearance down here? If nothing else except to help bring some sense of ease to an already paranoid town."

"Let me wrap up here tonight, catch my team up and I'll head out first thing in the morning. I should be there by tomorrow afternoon. I would prefer to stay in town rather than drive in when needed from the Springport office. Is there a place I can stay?"

"We have several bed and breakfasts in the area. I'll make arrangements for you. Will you be coming alone?"

"Yes. Thank you for booking my room. I will fax you a report tonight of my profile."

"Thanks for that Agent Hamilton. We appreciate any help we can get."

Chapter 31

The mayor was contemplating implementing a curfew and Sheriff Matthews agreed that would be an excellent idea. This may help some of the non-believers see the seriousness of the matter. Several women refused to believe that it could happen to them.

Sheriff Matthews stepped in front of the reporters once again.

"I would like to reach out again to the citizens of Hope and surrounding areas to please come forward if you notice any suspicious activity. No matter how insignificant you may think it is.

"Due to a third body found in such a short time, a curfew shall be implemented. We are insisting all women in the viewing area to please be home by nightfall. Keep your doors and windows locked at all times. Thank you."

"Do you still not have any suspects?"

"Is the killer leaving behind any clues?"

"I'm sorry, but no questions will be answered at this time," Sheriff Matthews stated firmly.

Chapter 32

Agent Alex Hamilton was ready to deplane. He had a super chatty neighbor that had refused to let him sleep. He stayed up most of the night finishing up what he needed to have completed for his team in Montana.

At least the local airport offered a car rental kiosk. He didn't even plan on turning on the radio. All he wanted was peace and quiet as he drove. It would give him time to regroup and gather his thoughts on this predator hunting the women of Hope and neighboring vicinities.

Once he had his rental car, he programmed the GPS and headed out. It was an hour ride, but he made better time than he thought he would.

The local Sheriff's Office was smaller than he expected. Now he understood why the state troopers had set up a mobile command center. Just to give them their own space.

* * *

Mindy, the receptionist, figured the man walking in the door had to be the profiler John was waiting for. He carried himself like an FBI agent. They were much easier to spot now. Unlike on the TV shows, she learned they didn't all wear black suits. He had a haggard look about him. It must have been a rough flight.

"You must be Agent Hamilton? I know Sheriff
Matthews will be glad you are here."

"Yes, I am. I'm afraid to ask how you know."

"I'm learning how to be more observant lately."

He laughed at her comment.

"I'll show you back. He is in his office."

"John, this is Agent Hamilton."

"I'm so glad you could make it. Rough flight?"

"I've had better."

"Let me introduce you to my team. This is Detectives
Johnson and Sanders."

***

Alex's jaw dropped when he saw Detective Sanders. He
couldn't believe his eyes; Sanders was gorgeous. She
looked to be in her mid to late 20's.

She was physically fit with a nicely tanned body. What
he wouldn't give to find out if she had any tan lines.

She had luscious lips that begged to be kissed. A head
full of curly auburn hair that he would love to tangle
his fingers in and the bluest eyes he had ever seen.
What a combination.

"Pleased to meet everyone. Could we have a moment alone Sheriff before we have a team meeting?"

"My office is this way," Sheriff Matthews said. "Son, you may want to pick up your jaw and roll your tongue back into your mouth. It has hit the floor." He said laughingly.

"That's Detective Sanders? She isn't anything like I pictured. Definitely not like any of the detectives I've worked with in the past."

"Yep. Don't let her looks fool you; she's a damn good one too. She could kick your ass, if needed. She's even a crack shot. She can out shoot most of the other deputies."

"I must say I'm intrigued."

"I don't want you to go breaking her heart. She's just like a daughter to me. I won't have any funny business, you hear. She's not something you can use just to help pass time."

"Yes, sir, I completely understand." Alex was also thinking that Detective Sanders was a big girl and could make her own decisions. The way she carried herself fascinated him immensely. He definitely wanted to get to know her better.

Sheriff Matthews hollered out his door, "Sanders and Johnson get your butts in here."

Sanders made sure to grab the case file before heading

in.

Sheriff Matthews stated matter of factly, "Sanders is the lead detective on the case."

* * *

Agent Hamilton had a certain presence about him. He appeared authoritative just standing there. Sanders wasn't sure if it was his build, height or both. His movements did not match with someone as tall and muscular as he was.

When they shook hands, Jordan felt an instant chemistry. She wondered if he felt it too. By the look in his eyes, he did.

She couldn't help but stare. She tried to look away, but couldn't. Damn, why did he have to be so good looking?

"You aren't planning on profiling us too, are you?"

"No, just this unsub. That way if any other murders happen, we may have a better understanding from the killer's point of view. It may help us solve the case faster if we have an idea of what went through the perp's mind. Or at least that's the thinking behind it anyway. I say each person is different. That's why there are so many psychopaths out there."

"Detective Sanders has also been trying to get into the mind of the killer."

Agent Hamilton stated, "I'm impressed with the work you've done in handling the cases. Not even some well-seasoned detectives are good at containing crime scenes. They like to move things to get closer to the body and can destroy footprints."

"Thanks. I tend to read all the books I can on forensics and crime scene investigation. I've also attended quite a few lectures that the state police and the FBI have offered. They say knowledge is power. I just never thought I would actually use it," Jordan explained.

"Again, I'm impressed with your work so far. You even crisscrossed the rubber bands over the booties. It gave your footprints a clear distinction. I'm quite surprised you had booties readily available."

"I keep a small crime scene kit in the trunk of my cruiser. I never had the need to use the booties until now. I primarily use the latex gloves, fingerprint kit, and the camera. The main crimes here are an occasional burglary, some domestic disturbances and bar room brawls. It's actually a peaceful town.

"I had figured the state trooper's crime scene unit would come in with booties also. I wanted to be able to differentiate my footprints from theirs. Plus any the perp may have left behind. If you go by the shoe prints, it would seem we have different perps. But the signature is always the same. I suspect that he is trying to throw us off by wearing different sized shoes."

Agent Hamilton agreed. "It's harder to get an estimate on height and weight with the different size shoes. I also suspect that he may be putting some kind of weights in the larger shoes. But then again, it is difficult to distinguish which ones are the larger shoes."

Out of the blue, Agent Hamilton asked, "Sheriff is there a good restaurant nearby? I very seldom make it to south Louisiana and want to enjoy some local cuisine. Some of my favorites are jambalaya, crawfish etouffée, gumbo, shrimp stew, red beans and rice with corn bread, and bread pudding for dessert. Oh, and how can I forget about boiled crabs and crawfish."

Sheriff Matthews laughed. "I guess you aren't too picky then. There is a local place, Rosy's Diner, nearby. Tonight's special is stuffed soft-shell crab topped with crawfish etouffée. The food there is *c'est bon*."

"Rosy's sounds perfect."

"The scenery is gorgeous too. It overlooks the little bayou in this town. The restaurant also shows the town's history. Every year Hope has a Civil War reenactment. The owner even has several artifacts and pictures to remind the locals of their history."

"Detective Sanders," asked Agent Hamilton, "Would you like to discuss the case in a little more detail over supper? I'm famished and want to eat something before looking over the case files. I will lose my appetite if I continue talking about this case."

"I haven't had much to eat today. *Allons*, let's go."

Sheriff Matthews teased them. "If I hadn't promised my wife I would be home for supper I'd join you. She's nagging about never seeing me. And even that's not true since we both work here."

Jordan shot him a look that said his company wasn't welcome.

Johnson joined in, "Yeah, I wish I could join you and talk about the case, but my wife would kill me if I went to eat out at Rosy's after she has been stuck in the house all day with the kids. Maybe I can call her to find a sitter though."

Jordan couldn't believe these two. "Go ahead and ask her Johnson. I'm sure she wants to listen to us talk about murder all night."

"No, that's ok. That would kill even my appetite. Besides, I'm hoping to get some alone time with my wife tonight."

Jordan wanted to get a feel for Agent Hamilton. She wanted, no needed, sex bad. She tried to stay away from the local men. In small towns people liked to talk way too much. Besides, most men here wanted a committed relationship. There was no such thing as a one night stand around this town. That's all she needed right now. Plus sex helped to clear her mind.

Rosy's was an old grocery store turned restaurant. In the center of the restaurant was a huge brick fireplace with seating all the way around. The wood floors had been restored to its natural sheen. Soft music played in

the background to give it a relaxing feeling. Various
civil war memorabilia decorated the walls. The outer
brick walls had even been restored. You could tell the
owner really embraced the history of the place.

It was a seat yourself restaurant. It had a homey feel
to it and could tell that it was a favorite with the locals.

They chose a table toward the back. With the news
media in town, this place was busy.

After finishing their meal and some small talk, Jordan
looked deeply into Agent Hamilton's eyes. "Would you
like to come over for a nightcap? No strings attached. I
just figured after flying all day you'd want to unwind.
We can go over the case files some more at my place."

He looked at her hard for a minute. This could get
messy, but then again she may just mean a night cap.

"Ok. Besides, I'm not sure exactly where I'm staying."

Jordan gave him directions to her house. "The bed and
breakfast is right down the road. We will pass it on the
way."

***

"What's your pleasure?" Jordan asked as they got to
her house.

"I'll take a beer if you have it."

"Beer it is."

Hamilton looked around. Not a bad little house. Small, quaint.

"It's not much to look at but the rent is cheap and the electricity is next to nothing. I couldn't stay living with my parents forever. Do you mind if I get out of these work clothes? " Jordan asked.

"Go ahead."

"Make yourself comfortable."

What should she wear? She didn't want to come off as desperate. She also needed to take a quick shower. It had been a long day at the office and she felt the dirtiness of the case on her.

She decided to wear a pair of sweat pants and T-shirt. Not romantic, but not desperate looking either.

She dashed into the bathroom to freshen up. The house had one bedroom and one bathroom. The bath was attached to the living room and bedroom. She closed the door to the main part of the house before undressing.

When she stepped into her room, she found Alex looking around. Clearing his throat, he stared at her body.

"I hope I didn't misread the signals?"

"No, you didn't. I wasn't sure if we were getting them

crossed. I thought perhaps you weren't interested."

It took all of two seconds for him to close the gap between them.

"You seem to have me at a disadvantage. You're already undressed. I could stare at your breasts all day. Especially now that I know what is hidden under that shirt."

"You don't just have to look, you can touch too."

The raw passion in his kisses took her breath away. No sense in wasting any time. She undressed him as they staggered over to the bed.

As soon as he stepped out of his pants she pushed him onto the bed. Her hands wandered over his body. Their hands roamed, caressed, and explored; neither could stop touching the other.

She slowly mounted him with a smile forming across her face. She wanted to kiss every inch of his body.

When she took him into her mouth, she thought he would lose complete control. Her tongue licked the tip of his erection and explored all around.

He flipped her on her back. "It's my turn now. You are going to make me cum before you've had any pleasure. You are a vixen."

He started with her breasts; sucking and teasing. She moaned in sheer pleasure.

"More, more. Oh, don't stop."

He trailed down her body with hot kisses. She'd had several lovers, but never one this enthusiastic.

He kept moving down. He let his tongue slip in and out, exploring, tasting. She pulled him up to her and wrapped her legs around him and opened up completely for him.
She was losing control and liked it. When they climaxed at the same time, Jordan was completely and truly satisfied.

Alex's voice was husky when he said, "That was incredible."

"Mm hmm, isn't that usually the woman's line? You were unbelievable. I'm still floating on cloud nine. I don't think I've ever had such an orgasmic pleasure before."

Laughing, he snuggled up to her. "Guess I'll have to try to break my own record then."

"Please stay the night."

"I'm not going anywhere."

"I want you to know I'm not some starry-eyed female. I'm not looking for love at first sight, or love period. Just some fun."

"Good to know. Now rest up for round two." After

kissing, they curled up together and fell sound asleep.

For the first time since the bodies were discovered, she dreamed about something other than death.

Chapter 33

Sheriff Matthews walked into the house and threw his jacket over a chair. He grabbed a beer from the fridge while unbuttoning his shirt. This job was getting to him, or in all honesty it was this case.

The town was a ghost town now. Everyone stayed inside with their doors locked as much as possible. He knew people looked at him and thought he wasn't doing enough to keep them protected or the town safe. That awful feeling continuously ate away at him.

He heard Mindy upstairs getting ready for bed. She was his one constant in life right now. Slowly he made his way upstairs, trying to ease the stress from his body. He didn't know what he would do without her.

Chapter 34

The night was quiet, too quiet. The stillness wore on his nerves. He needed the screams to fill the house, to keep the quiet from closing in on him. Pure, animalistic need drove him tonight. The need to make his prey scream, to feel the blood on his skin. He had to inflict pain on someone so he wouldn't remember the pain of his childhood. He had to punish someone.

It was time to go hunting. He smiled. The anticipation of the hunt and capture began to turn him on. He couldn't wait to get her back here and restrain her. Bringing her fear and pain from the torture he would put her through. Listening to her screams and pleas. She would be begging for death before it was over.

Out here she could scream and beg all she wanted. No one would hear her; no one would come to help her. The whore would get what she deserved, punishment and humiliation. She would become another masterpiece he had created.

After finding a secluded parking spot, he kept to the shadows and waited for his next masterpiece. He caught the woman's scent before he saw her, the cloying scent of her perfume. That mixed with the sexuality that exuded from her very presence was intoxicating.

It was getting late for someone to be out in the park alone. Obviously she wasn't worried about the serial killer loose in Hope. Thankfully not everyone took heed to Sheriff Matthews' warning.   The svelte woman immediately enticed him with her alluring walk. She had a nice bronze tan, one that could only come from a tanning bed.

As he let his imagination wander, he noticed she had a tennis bag over a shoulder and was heading to the tennis courts. The Hunter didn't see anyone else, so he hoped that she didn't plan to meet up with anyone. He would wait for the opportune moment to make sure he went unnoticed when he abducted her.

***

Danielle opened her eyes to see her image looking back at her. The room was covered floor to ceiling with mirrors. She felt as if a heavy fog clouded her head. She was strapped to some kind of chair and couldn't move. There were other various restraints in the room also.

She tried to scream, but her mouth refused to open.

Where was she? How did she get here? How long had she even been here? The last thing Danielle Taylor remembered was leaving the house to play a quick game of tennis. She preferred to play tennis at night, while the park was empty. It was as if she had her own private course. It was also cheaper than a gym membership. Her husband, Mike, would watch the kids so she could slip away for a bit of peace and quiet.

She cringed in fear when she heard footsteps coming closer. Her blood turned to ice as the door opened and a man entered. He was naked except for the surgical gloves.

He laughed at her as she attempted to recoil from his touch.

She heard someone talking to her, but it was difficult to make out what he was saying. She had a hard time pushing the pain in her mouth aside.

"I'm glad you are finally awake. I had such a hard time waiting for you to wake up. I worked on your mouth while you were asleep, but I must work on your eyes now that you are awake."

Her captor bent over her in deep concentration. She felt the super glue as he applied it to her eyelids.

The pain was horrendous as warm blood oozed from the wounds he caused. She lost count of the different tools he had used on her. She was on autopilot. Her mind attempted to block everything out.

As the knife slipped into her skin, her surroundings faded around her as the room went black and she passed out.

She heard someone yelling at her. Suddenly she felt a stinging sensation across her face. Her mind was sluggish. She had never been good at handling pain. Her pain threshold was relatively low.

"Now this just won't do, I can't have you constantly passing out on me. We won't get anything done. I want you to play with me."

Danielle tried to recall how she got herself into this situation. She remembered vaguely waking up and lying on a van floor. Hearing a man's laughter taunting her, telling her it's not time to wake up. Then it felt like electricity had coursed through her body, as if being shocked. Now she was here listening to the cruelest laughter she'd ever heard.

All her life she was considered stubborn, a fighter. Now she was ready to let the darkness consume her. She was ready for death to take her away from this place. She was so cold, so very cold.

Chapter 35

Mike was worried about Danielle. She should have been home by now. The most she stayed out was an hour.

She was always home to tuck the kids into bed. He'd been trying her cell phone, but it just rang. Mike called 911.

"911, what is your emergency?"

"This is Mike Taylor. My wife should have been home from Lakeview Park almost two hours ago. She isn't answering her cell phone and I'm worried about her. I'd go look for her, but I hate to wake up the kids."

"Mr. Taylor, I'm going to send a patrol car over to the park. What does your wife drive?"

"She has an olive green Land Rover."

***

"Dispatch, we are at Lakeview Park. The Land Rover is in the parking lot. Unfortunately, there is no sign of Mrs. Taylor. You better send backup and the crime scene unit. A memo had been distributed to be on the lookout for missing women. Supposedly there is a serial killer in a neighboring town, who likes to hunt outside of his kill zone. You may want to touch base with them."

The 911 dispatcher called the City of Hope's

dispatcher. "The state trooper's office over here is working on a missing person's case. No details as of yet."

"Thank you. I'll let our team here know."

The dispatcher hated to be the one to wake everyone up. She said a quick Novena that this wasn't their killer striking again.

"Sheriff, Montouy called in a missing person alert. I just received notification from the state trooper dispatcher. No details yet."

"Hopefully it is not our guy."

"From your mouth to God's ears."

"I'll call Sanders and inform her. I'm sure she'll at least want to be aware of the fact. Thanks Drew."

***

Sanders was drifting off to sleep when the blasted cell phone rang. "Sanders speaking, what happened?"

"Missing person in Montouy. I am going to head over and see what's up. Did you want to ride over with me?"

"Give me ten minutes."

"The crime scene techs are on their way out. They should be there shortly. Maybe they will come up with something."

***

It had been a long heart wrenching night. The young mom's tennis bag had been found, but nothing else. Another woman seemed to have disappeared into thin air. Jordan feared that they would be finding another body soon.

She called Johnson, "Johnson, I didn't want to wake you earlier, but Montouy has a young mother of two missing. She went to play tennis before bed and never came home. We need to arrange a higher level of patrols. If this is our guy, he will be disposing of yet another body in the next day or so."

"I'll get to work on it right away. I'll also call Deputy Williams and have him stake out the roads coming into town. If he is driving his white utility van, maybe we can get the SOB."

"That's a great idea. Let's try it."

Jordan looked over at Sheriff Matthews and said, "Johnson is calling Deputy Williams to start a stakeout for the white van. Maybe we will get lucky and he is driving it with a body inside."

Chapter 36

The Hunter used his dad's old suburban for hunting tonight. He knew it would be better to swap out vehicles. The back windows had been tinted and the carpet removed. A secret compartment had been fitted with restraints for the hands and feet. Everything was tucked away nicely.

The Hunter had to be careful and meticulous to continue killing. He attempted to keep each victim alive longer than the last. He seemed to be stuck at 48 hours for a victim enduring the torture. He hoped to eventually get up to 72 hours.

The storm began to pick up outside. The lightning came straight down and the thunder was rolling continuously. Tonight's weather provided the perfect cover to dispose of the body. No one would be out in weather like this.

Each masterpiece seemed to be improving. Rosedale Antebellum Home would be having their birthday celebration tomorrow, complete with a fun jump and games for the kids.

He'd never met a woman who wanted to miss a good time; this one would be no exception. The tricky part would be going unnoticed down that road. They kept the entryway lit up at night.

Chapter 37

Terry Rouchon wanted the birthday celebration at Rosedale to go off without a hitch. He had only been grounds manager for eight months, but he knew how important it was to keep the grounds looking nice for this event. It could mean his job if something went wrong.

This celebration was one of their main advertisers. The grounds and some areas of the home were rented out for weddings, banquets, and functions. Claire Rosedale had started sending out invitations almost as soon as that year's celebration transpired to past visitors, newspapers, bridal magazines, whoever she thought of. This was a huge deal for Rosedale.

The entryway to Rosedale always took his breath away. In his opinion, this was one of the most dramatic antebellum homes in the area. The brick and wrought iron fence ran along the entire length of the front. Ancient oak trees covered in moss lined the drive. From the road, you could still make out the grand home, with its large six white columns supporting both the first and second floor. All six of the elegant double doors were recently sanded and stained to give them a regal look. Terry even had someone come in and repaint the house a pristine white.

The bayou ran along the back of the plantation giving homage to its true southern heritage. Two large sugar cane plots had been added to each side of the grounds. Water fountains were placed in each one with vibrant red knockout rose bushes planted around them. Terry even made sure the brick walkway leading up to the home had been pressure washed.

He was proud of himself. Everything seemed to be perfect. That was until he went to check the sign announcing Rosedale Antebellum Home and when it was founded.

From a distance, it appeared that only one light remained burning.

"Oh sweet Jesus." Terry couldn't believe his eyes; propped up against the sign was a body.

He got back into his truck and headed to the main house to call 911.

"This is Terry Rouchon. You need to get someone over here at Rosedale. There's a body right at the entrance way sign."

"I'm dispatching a patrol car and the detectives right now. Please don't touch anything."

"No worries there."

***

The dispatcher called Detective Sanders first, "I already dispatched a patrol car, but we have a dead body at Rosedale. Did you want to call the Sheriff?"

"That's fine. Let the crime scene techs know. You may have to give them directions."

Jordan turned to Alex, "Our dead body made its appearance at Rosedale. They have a big celebration planned for today too."

"Let's go. Guess we'll take two separate cars since I'll want to follow the body."

"Okay. I still haven't been able to make an appearance at an autopsy."

***

The air had a smell of decaying flesh. The beauty of Rosedale was postcard perfection except for the mutilated body left at the sign announcing the antebellum home.

Deputy Williams greeted her, "I didn't check the body. I was waiting for the crime scene techs and coroner to get here."

Jordan called the Sheriff to give him an update. "Sheriff, I believe Mrs. Taylor is no longer missing. I think the body left at Rosedale's entrance is hers. Crime scene techs are on their way."

"I'm heading out. Ms. Rosedale has already called the mayor. She is worried about her celebration."

Jordan hung up and asked Alex, "Impressions?"

"He is escalating. Same signature, almost the same mutilation of the body. He is all over the place with the time between kills.”

The coroner pulled up along with the crime scene techs. “We have to stop meeting like this.   She’s still warm, hasn’t been dead long. He cleaned her thoroughly with what smells like bleach and looks like acid.”

“I’ll try to locate her dental records for you.”

“Appreciate it.”

Chapter 38

It was after lunch before they could all meet in the conference room to discuss today's recent murder. You could smell the food as soon as you walked into the station.

Someone was thoughtful enough to bring by a slow cooker full of red beans, sausage and rice for them. Agent Hamilton even spotted homemade cornbread.

There was also boudin and cracklins. He hated to admit it, but he was addicted to the boudin that people dropped off at the Sheriff's office. He might have to bring some back home with him. There was nothing like south Louisiana to him. It had it all, the hospitality, charm and food.

"Sheriff, do you always get fed like this?"

"What do you mean?"

"Is it because of the case or is all this food normal?"

"Someone is always dropping off something for us to eat it seems. I never really thought about it, but it is a big help with all of us working so hard right now," the sheriff answered.

"It must be nice. I'm used to going all day without eating when working on a big case. I'm not used to someone bringing in food."

"You're just not working a case in the right place then,

son. There's nothing like good ole southern hospitality."

"I can't argue with you there I guess."

Alex looked around at the somber faces, "This latest victim had only been missing overnight. The unsub is all over the place with a time frame; that concerns me. Only he knows what it is. I haven't been able to predict when he will strike next."

Jordan informed the group, "I heard from the lab, there was no forensic evidence found."

Victim

Sarah Metzger
DM – October 2
DOD – October 3
Carpet fibers from possible Ford van

Marilyn Hennessey
DM – November 3
DOD – November 5
No trace evidence found on/near body

Andrea Smith
DM – November 20
DOD – November 23
Trace amount of semen found on the body

Whitney Guillory
DM – December 5
DOD – December 8

Danielle Taylor
DM – December 15
DOD – December 16

Location

Undetermined
Secluded

Isolated
Possible hunting camp ????

Unsub

Mid 30's
Possibly drives Ford van, possibly white in color
Caucasian
6 feet, plus ???
Well-built
In shape
Financially well off
Sexual dysfunction

Personality

Cunning
Superiority complex

Method of Killing

Torture
Rape/sexual assault: pre and post mortem
Breast mutilation
Cleaning body after death with bleach and acid

Chapter 39

The original gas lights still lined Main Street of Hope. Over the years they had been modernized to increase efficiency, but also still keeping the same look. The old fashioned lights gave Main Street a soft, peaceful glow at night.

The town had great success a while back doing a fundraiser for a community center. At first, there had been a lot of opposition. Several members of the community considered it an unnecessary expense. Now they all felt that the town couldn't survive without it. It gave the kids something to do on school breaks besides causing trouble.

The community center was originally an old hospital, then a school. Left abandoned for years, it soon became another town eyesore. When the new Mayor was elected, he formed a committee to do something about the eyesores in town. The community center transformed into one of the main focal points as you came into town. It no longer looked like a rundown building, but something bursting with life.

The front area of the first floor was rented out for parties. There was talk of adding a play and picnic area to the exterior. The proceeds from the carnival would be used for this particular expansion.

An arcade had been added to the second floor, and the top floor was renovated into a laser tag game that wrapped down to the back and down to the old basement. This was a huge success with the teenagers. Last year a haunted house even opened up in the laser tag section during Halloween.

Chapter 40

The urge was building; he needed the rush from the thrill of the kill. He shouldn't go after another local girl tonight, but the need overpowered him. He shouldn't be hunting this close to his last kill. The last one died too fast though, he needed this bad.

Besides, no one knew The Hunter's identity. He had been careful and hadn't made a *faux pas* yet.

Hope High School had just completed construction on a new track. Several of the teachers made use of it with the killer running loose. They felt more comfortable running there than on the road.

The Hunter knew once the bell rang most of the teachers and students cleared out. This may be the perfect time to hunt. The rain had cleared up so only the dedicated runners would be out.

***

The weather had just cleared when Erica Singley started her run. With no one around, she didn't have to worry about idle chit chat. She enjoyed teaching, but the stress of the killings was wearing on all of the teachers' nerves. It's all they wanted to talk about, especially since the first victim had been a teacher at the nearby private school. Erica was glad Christmas break was finally here, and looked forward to two weeks of doing absolutely nothing.

Erica had just celebrated her 30th birthday and noticed

a few gray hairs showing up in her dark brown hair. She had to make a hair appointment soon. She still wasn't ready to accept her age, even though Joseph, her husband of six years, reassured her that she was still beautiful.

Erica was jogging along to the music when she felt her head snap back. Then a hand was covering her mouth. Erica refused to go down without a fight. She attempted to push the rag away or at least bite her attacker. However, her struggling seemed to cause the drugs to kick in faster and she couldn't fight the darkness that was overcoming her.

***

Her heart pounded as she opened her eyes. Her brain didn't want to cooperate at all. She swore she was in a moving vehicle of some sort. As things became clearer, she became certain she was in a van, but there didn't seem to be any covering on the floorboards, and her arms and legs were restrained to the floor. The flooring was cold and she could feel the indentations in the metal.

She tried to calm down and recall what had happened. She remembered running and arms grabbing her from behind. Then a damp cloth was placed over her nose and mouth. It had a sweet aroma to it. She recalled struggling and trying to kick her captor.

She didn't know how long she had been out or her location. It felt as if the van was traveling down a gravel road or at the very least a rough riding road.

But that didn't mean much. A lot of the roads around here weren't in the best of shape.

She pulled against the restraints. If only she could get out of the handcuffs.

"I see you are starting to wake up. We can't have that just yet."

She noticed an object of some sort in his hands. An electrical shock coursed through her body and blackness overcame her.

As she slipped into unconsciousness, she heard her captor's cold laughter. It sent fear rushing through her body.

***

As Erica woke up, she began to realize that she still couldn't move. Lying there cold and shivering, terror moved through her body. The fear was so strong it turned to ice water running through her veins. Her heart felt as if it would pound right out of her chest. She had trouble breathing. She told herself to remain calm. *Deep breaths. Focus. Observe your surroundings. You must open your eyes and focus. Above all else, stay calm! Panicking won't help you get out of whatever mess you have landed yourself in.*

Why couldn't she move? Suddenly she felt something cold prick her from behind.

As her eyes came into focus, she made out her image in the mirror. Oh, no! She really was in trouble. She was standing upright and strapped to some kind of bed frame. If she relaxed or leaned back it felt like tiny needles poking into her.

A figure appeared in the doorway. Something about him exuded darkness and evil. She desperately tried hard not to panic, but she found it extremely difficult to remain calm. Especially when everywhere you looked there were torture devices. Why in the world did he need the room completely mirrored?

"I thought I would try this one first seeing as you like to bite. The springs will bite into your backside ever so gently as I enjoy tormenting you from the front. When I believe you've had enough, we'll move on to something else."

She started to panic, but as she pulled away, she felt the bite of the metal. It took all that she had to not panic even further as her captor started to speak again.

"First things first though, we have to pull those teeth. This little device should be handy at keeping your head still."

She noticed the pliers in his hand and cringed. She was already on the verge of passing out from the pain of having her teeth pulled, when he started stitching her mouth closed.

When she came to she remained shackled to the spring contraption. Now she understood what the mirrors were for. He was forcing her to watch everything he did to her. He pried her eyes open so that she couldn't close them.

"Uh-uh. You aren't getting off that easy. It's not time for you to pass out again. Now, what shall we do next? I'm thinking of a special mani and pedi. I know how you women like to have your nails done."

The pain was something fierce. Her screams resonated through her head. *Heaven help me please.* Her hands and feet burned terribly. When she looked down, she saw they were a complete bloody mess.

As the pain became unbearable, terror gripped her. She wouldn't survive this ordeal. She prayed that he would kill her soon and get this over with.

He slapped her face hard, "I'm not ready for you to pass out just yet. We still have more things to do."

She couldn't help it and passed out. When she came to she had been moved. Now she was chained to the floor.

"On your knees now!"

Her body was slick from the blood, making it difficult to keep her balance. She did as he instructed. She didn't want to make him mad. Tears streamed down her face as he shoved her to where she was on all fours.

"You're going to be my bitch now. You are under my control and will do what I tell you to do."

She would eventually die, but how much more did she have to endure before he killed her?

He stroked her skin with some kind of whip. The leather felt cool against her skin. It had some kind of sharp studs attached to it.

His erection brushed up against her as he stroked her skin. Her body involuntarily shuddered from his touch. "Mm, see your body is telling me yes, even if you can't."

She wished she could tell him that it wasn't desire that made her shiver, but repulsion.

As he entered her, she felt the lashes of the whip against her skin. She tried to envision herself anywhere but here.

The pain was blinding. She prayed that she would pass out from it. She wanted this sheer torture to come to an end.

Blackness enveloped her. She felt him slap her face, but the pain had become too much for her to handle.

* * *

The docile women did not turn him on; the more fear they showed the harder he became. This one refused to show any emotion, no matter how much torturing he performed on her. Her mind had already given up and was in another place. This just wouldn't do.

He punished her brutally for biting him and bit her all over. He hid the bite marks under the welts from the whip since it managed to take off a good bit of her skin. He even seared some bite marks off with the butane torch. Those too deep to hide he dropped some acid on since it ate away the area perfectly.

He had a lot of fun teaching this one a lesson. A lesson she would never forget.

The Hunter looked down at his prey afterwards. "The whore. She was weak." The need was too great though, he couldn't control it. He had to keep going. Just this one time he would let himself lose complete control.

Chapter 41

Joseph had to put in six hours of overtime tonight. He forgot to call Erica to tell her that he would be working late and was surprised that she hadn't called asking where he was.

He tried her cell phone but she didn't answer. He decided to just pick up a quick bite to eat on the way home. Lately his hours had been pretty hectic so maybe she had figured out that he had to work late.

The local paper mill believed that they would save money by laying off the workers close to retirement. That had to be the lowest thing a company could do. Now, everyone was left scrambling to keep up with the demand. But at least the money was good and he needed the job. There just weren't many available in the local area.

As Joseph passed by the school, he noticed Erica's car still in the parking lot. They couldn't afford to purchase a new car right now and he hoped she didn't have car trouble because the house needed a new roof first.

By the time he arrived home, the house was bathed in darkness. When he opened the front door, the quietness took him by surprise. He couldn't believe Erica actually managed to turn the TV off before going to bed.

He tried to be quiet when he entered the bedroom but froze when he saw the bed was still made. After searching the house, Erica was nowhere to be found. Joseph called the sheriff's office.

"Hope Sheriff's Office, what is your emergency?"

"This is Joseph Singley; my wife is missing. She isn't home and I noticed when I drove by the school her car was still there."

"Mr. Singley, I'm going to send a patrol car over to the school. Do you think she may have had car trouble and left it there?"

"That was my thought, but if she isn't home, then where is she?"

***

Deputy Andrews called Detective Sanders. "You better get the crime scene techs over to Hope High. We have a possible abduction; another missing teacher. There are signs of a struggle. I found her shoes heading into the woods surrounding the track. It looks like she kicked them off."

"Will we ever catch a break? I'll get crime scene out there. You better call the sheriff," Jordan answered.

Deputy Andrews quickly called the sheriff, "Sheriff, we have another missing teacher. This one is from Hope High. I'm waiting for the team to get here. It appears she was abducted while running."

"Damn, why didn't she heed our warning?"

Chapter 42

The night was so clear you could see the stars in the sky. With the trees and moss swaying in the breeze, the bayou had an enchanted look about it. Every now and then an alligator or snake would bring a ripple in the water.

He used his night vision goggles to help guide him through the night. This way he wouldn't need to worry with lights on the boat. He knew these waters like the back of his hands, but he had to keep a lookout for any obstacles in the water.

With the sheriff's office upping patrols, he would have to be smarter than them to pose his masterpiece. The night was too quiet and still to use even the trolling motor on the boat. He didn't want to chance anyone noticing him out tonight. He would have to be careful paddling into town. It was a risky move, but the idea of slipping in right under their noses had him feeling superior.

He had checked the pirogue for damage the other day. He kept it hidden under a low hanging branch covered with moss on the bayou. It'd been in the water for over 24 hours and still hadn't sunk. He should be good.

The Community Center was such a joke; this town didn't care about its kids. He felt a need to punish this town for never suspecting his dad of abuse. Someone should have recognized the signs and helped him and his mom. But no, they all believed his dad to be an upstanding citizen. That or they were just too damned scared of him.

Besides, the Community Center needed one of his masterpieces. They claimed they loved to display local art, but none of his work was displayed there. Well, that was about to change. He would hand deliver a special work of art just for them and he wouldn't even charge.

This next piece in his series was perfect. They would be truly impressed.

The wide staircase leading up to the grand double doors was decorated for Christmas. It was just missing the one little detail. He laid out the red velvet material that would be the backdrop and carefully propped her up against the door. Perfect.

As he slipped away, he made sure no one was around to see him.

Chapter 43

Sheriff Matthews despised being woken up at 5:30 in the morning. What made it worse was that the day would start out with another homicide. Their killer had struck again.

The sun was starting to rise by the time everybody arrived at the crime scene. Thankfully, someone brought along some coffee.

Sheriff Matthews and the coroner had arrived at the same time. The coroner walked up to Jordan. "Detective Sanders, I'm considering setting me up a command center out here too. I can now drive here blindfolded. Let's go see what he left for us today."

"I'm right behind you."

"It appears that your killer has taken to cleaning the body carefully. I suspect he washed the body down with bleach and an acid of some sort. I will know more at autopsy."

Later that afternoon Jordan's Caller ID showed that it was the coroner's office calling. "Sanders. What do you have for me Doc?"

"Well, don't bother requesting dental records. You will need a DNA match. The SOB pulled all her teeth out."

"What? That's new. He loves to step up the game."

＊

The victims appear to be random. The only similarity seemed to be that they vanished into thin air.

He didn't seem to kill out of lust or sexual fantasy, although there was sexual assault to the latest bodies. Instead, he killed out of need, as if to humiliate the women. The first two victims had been raped with objects, most likely a knife.

This killer indeed had a severely warped mind. In the deep recesses of his mind lay a very twisted sexual fantasy. But what fed that fantasy?

They had no clues as to how he selected his victims much less disposed of their bodies. He may even be coming into town by the bayou as well as the road. That would mean he had some serious physique. A dead body was heavier than one would imagine. It wasn't an easy task to carry a body through town in the middle of the night. They would need to start patrolling the shoreline as well. There were only a limited number of deputies as it was and everyone was already getting burned out. Maybe the state troopers could help with surveillance.

Each crime scene they investigated was like déjà vu. The severity of the torture increased but all the forensic reports read the same. No trace evidence was found. He made sure there were no fingertips, including nails for any skin to get caught under. No DNA evidence had shown up except for minuscule amounts. There was no match in CODIS to help identify the perp.

Up until now the killer had always shown an amazing amount of control. The bodies had never shown this amount of carnage.

What the hell would drive someone to commit this kind of torture on another person? There was truly a sinister person lurking about.

He forced each of these victims to watch their own death. At least, that was the detectives' reasoning behind the eyes being pried open.

These killings seem to be triggered on impulse. Even though the killings were very methodical, there was no set timeline. He killed when he felt the need.

Unfortunately, the need seemed to be increasing. The kills appeared to be organized, but spontaneous. He had to be a single man, with no neighbors. Surely if he lived in a neighborhood someone would have heard or at least seen something.

Jordan was updating the murder board when Agent Hamilton walked in. "This perp didn't allow any time between kills this time. It's not even a weekend. He must not have a day to day job to worry with."

"That or he is unemployed."

Agent Hamilton looked at her deep in thought. "How many people are financially stable here not to work?"

"I don't know. I've never even thought of it. I don't

think there would be that many though. It's not like
we have too many self-made millionaires here," she
answered.

"Until now I figured he worked shift work or at least
had the weekends off. With the time frame he is
killing in though, I am leaning towards the fact that he
might be unemployed or at least financially stable
enough where he doesn't have to work."

"Sheriff may know better than me. It's worth following
up on though. Unfortunately, in this economy, there
are quite a few unemployed residents at this time."

"He isn't disabled because he has to carry the bodies.
A dead body is not as light as one would think."

Murder Board

Victim

Sarah Metzger
DM – October 2
DOD – October 3
Carpet fibers from possible Ford van

Marilyn Hennessey
DM – November 3
DOD – November 5
No trace evidence found on/near body

Andrea Smith

DM – November 20
DOD – November 23
Trace amount of semen found on the body

Whitney Guillory
DM – December 5
DOD – December 8

Danielle Taylor
DM – December 15
DOD – December 16

Erica Singley
DM = December 21
DOD – December23

Location

Undetermined
Secluded
Isolated
Possible hunting camp ????

Unsub

Mid 30's
Possibly drives Ford van, possibly white in color
Caucasian
6 feet, plus ???
Well-built
In shape
Financially well off or unemployed
Sexual dysfunction

Personality

Cunning
Superiority complex

Method of Killing

Torture
Rape/sexual assault: pre and post mortem
Breast mutilation
Cleaning body after death with bleach and acid

Chapter 44

Sheriff Matthews stepped in front of the reporters once again. Today, he had to confirm that there had been another murder, but nothing else.

"I'm just going to make a general statement to the public, that's it. No questions will be answered. This is NOT a press conference. Yes, another body has been discovered, and has not been identified. It is believed to be another homicide.

"We are stressing that all women in the viewing area please be careful. Do not venture out after dark by yourself. Be aware of your surroundings, even during the day."

The reporters, of course, didn't listen and started spouting off questions.

"Do you have any suspects as of yet?"

"Do you have any clues?"

"I'm sorry, but no questions will be answered at this time. This is an open investigation." Sheriff answered, feeling like a broken record.

Chapter 45

Jordan could feel a migraine coming on. This case was turning into a living hell. Not just for Jordan, but for everyone involved. All she wanted to do was crawl into a hot bubble bath and soak. She wanted a few minutes to herself, without thinking about the case.

She turned on the local radio station after she started up her car. Maybe listening to music would help ease her nerves. But during the commercial break, all the DJ talked about was the recent murders. That idea was a bust and she quickly turned off the radio. *So much for a bit of peace and quiet.*

Her thoughts were interrupted when her cell phone rang. "Where are you?" Alex asked.

"On my way home, I have a bubble bath calling my name."

"I just left the state troopers' command center. Do you feel like some company? I give a mean massage."

"Sounds perfect, I have a headache starting. This case is getting to me. I'll leave the back door open for you."

"You'll do no such thing. In case you've forgotten, there is a serial killer stalking women in this town. Besides, I'm right behind you." As if to prove that fact he flashed his lights at her.

"If you are right behind me, then why'd you ask where I was?" she asked before hanging up the phone, with a smile on her face.

Chapter 46

The Hunter smiled to himself. These hick cops were so insignificant to him. He had the state troopers and FBI stumped as well.

A smile slowly crept across his face as he watched the news. It still remained vague on his masterpieces, but Sheriff Matthews didn't look like he was having a good day. He rather enjoyed the fact he continued to cause the sheriff and other law enforcement such mass confusion. He brought all the personnel such stress in their lives. They were working round the clock just because of him and getting nowhere.

The next morning he immediately went out to purchase several newspapers. The newspapers still didn't include a picture of his latest masterpiece on the front page but they did have a picture of the crime scene. That would have to do for now. He did, however, notice a female cop working the scene.

"Now how did I miss this? I never realized the town had a female cop. This could be fun."

A plan began to take form in his mind. She would be the perfect prey, but first a trap had to be laid out. A little hide and seek game would be fun with her.

Chapter 47

Jordan heard Mindy calling after her, "Detective Sanders, you have some mail delivered. It says for your eyes only."

Jordan inspected the envelope and saw no return address. This couldn't be good. Even worse, it was postmarked Springport, it was so busy there, nobody would remember a single letter. Plus there were so many drop off points that it would be useless to explore that avenue. There would also be numerous fingerprints on the envelope, so that would be pointless as well. Then again, it could be nothing.

"Hold on Mindy. I'm going to get some gloves and an evidence bag just in case."

Jordan asked Johnson and the Sheriff to come over as well, just in case it did turn out to be something.

They stood around while she carefully opened the envelope. Taking a pencil she took extreme care in opening the piece of paper that slid out.

"How did you like my current masterpiece?"
Signed
The Hunter

The Sheriff looked at her, "This can't be good. He has decided to communicate with you and he hunts women."

"What do you think he means by masterpiece? Does

he actually think these bodies are works of art? Plus, he has named himself The Hunter. I don't have a good feeling about this Sheriff."

"Neither do I, I'm going to call the FBI. We also need to give the profiler a call and ask him to head over here. He mentioned earlier that he wanted to check out the locations where the bodies were found."

Jordan just stood there lost in thought while the Sheriff called Agent Hamilton. "Detective Sanders received a letter for her eyes only from the unsub. He has named himself The Hunter and calls the carnage he left behind his masterpieces."

"I'm not far from there. I want to take a close look at the letter before it is sent off to the lab. The state troopers will send someone to pick up the letter so that it can be analyzed. Maybe they can retrieve some trace evidence from it. Surveillance needs to be put on Sanders ASAP."

***

Agent Hamilton walked into the Sheriff's Office later on that day. Wasting no time, he asked, "Do you still have the letter?"

"Yep, it's right here. It appears to be pretty generic. I doubt that we will get any evidence off of it," the sheriff explained.

"I've been keeping my team briefed on your case. We have been working on several theories. Now that he has made contact this may be just the break we need.

I suspect that these murders weren't his first. I believe he has been murdering for quite some time," Alex explained.

"How is it that no bodies have been found until now? Even the FBI database didn't get any hits."

"He probably has been careful, concealing the bodies. Possibly experimenting at first."

"So, why is he disposing the bodies out in the open?" The sheriff asked confused.

"I'm willing to bet he wanted to step up his game. He may even be getting bored. Worse, he could need more stimulation.

Chapter 48

The need to hunt, to kill, came rushing through him like a tidal wave. He felt a stirring in his groin as he planned out his next hunt.

The Hunter truly enjoyed hunting. His murderous thoughts were dark; the need to hunt consumed him. He ached to see the blood on his hands, to see the fear in her eyes. The anticipation sent tingles through his body. A sinister smile crept across his face as his eyes turned black as coal and the evil took over his soul.

He headed out to hunt when he noticed someone walking alongside the road. As he got closer, there was no mistaking it was a woman. Before he made his move, he checked to make sure no headlights were headed his way.

He couldn't believe his luck when he pulled over to talk with the woman.

"Need a ride?"

"My stupid boyfriend kicked me out of the car. He's such an asshole. I wasn't even looking at the guy and he gets all pissy."

As she spoke, The Hunter could smell the alcohol on her, she actually reeked of it.

"Hop in. It's not safe to walk around out here by yourself. You know there is talk of a serial killer roaming the streets."

"Thanks dude. I'm Sam Harrington by the way."

A grin crossed his face in the darkness as he replied, "I'm Hunter."

The night was definitely picking up. What perfect luck; his prey found him tonight. They weren't far from The Hideaway either.

She would also help with all the urges he had been feeling for *mon douce* Detective. He couldn't wait for the day he hunted Detective Sanders. He wanted to feel her racing heartbeat, see the fear in her eyes when he took her. He wanted to hear her screams as he whipped her while thrusting into her deeply.

This one would have to do. He was already planning which tortures he would do. He would force her to kneel before him and take him into her mouth. All the while he knew it would be the sweet Detective's face he would be imagining. Desire raced through his body as his erection twitched in anticipation.

***

Blood oozed from the body where numerous welts from the whip had hit. He had her shackled to the wall which allowed him to whip her from the front or back. As much as he enjoyed his chair, it was difficult to reach their backside with it. He wanted his art to start showing full dimension.

He was also considering the addition of a branding iron

of some sort instead of using just the cigarettes and butane torch. He may have to increase his hunting time, there were so many techniques and not enough victims to try them on. He could no longer wait so long in between hunts. He just had to continue being careful so the cops had no clue as to his identity.

Even after he savagely whipped her, she continued to struggle and attempt to free herself. He retrieved a poker from the fireplace and heated it up. Looking at her, he envisioned all of the places he could brand. It may even make the perfect sex toy to use, after he had another go at her.

As he moved closer to her, she screamed out in sheer terror. He had not yet sewn her mouth shut and would have to do it soon. She was bleary eyed but still had some fight hidden in those eyes.

"Scream all you want, *mon cher*. No one can hear you. No one will come to your rescue."

After branding her, he used the pliers to pull her teeth before sealing her mouth shut. Then the fun really began.

This one didn't disappoint him one bit. Maybe it was all the alcohol, but he swore at times she actually enjoyed it. She kept letting out sexy little moans instead of screams. Once he even felt her climax.

He became totally lost in the moment, imagining that she was *mon douce* Detective. When he regained some self-control he found himself covered in blood.

His rage took over as time stood still. How could he be so careless? He slashed the body more than he wanted and didn't give himself time to live out his fantasy with the Detective. He had to work on regaining his self-control with his next victim. He wanted full control when he finally brought *mon douce* Detective back here to enjoy.

The arousal that he felt while torturing the girl remained. She was still alive, but barely. He quickly finished off his fantasy. As he climaxed he screamed out the Detective's name over and over.

Now that he was spent, he cleaned up the body. He had to make sure he left behind no evidence, including bite marks. He had learned from his past mistake of waiting because it became extremely difficult to maneuver the body once rigor had set it.

There was still some time left before sunrise. If he hurried, he could pose this masterpiece before daylight.

He placed the body in the bed of the truck and headed out. He decided to pose her right on Main Street by a gas lamp. But there would be no time to make sure she was perfect.

He couldn't believe his luck as he watched the sheriff's car turned off and the street was now deserted. Moving quickly, he propped her up and headed back to his camp.

In his rear-view mirror he could make out the body.
Even for a quick pose, the masterpiece looked perfect.

Chapter 49

Joe Thomas was running late for work as usual. He sure hoped no one from the sheriff's office was running radar this early in the morning. He knew they were stepping up patrol with this maniac running loose.

As he was about to turn down a side street, something caught his eye. At first he thought someone may have been injured, but as he got closer, he knew just how wrong he was.

He reached into his shirt pocket and took out his phone. He called 911 without even getting out of his truck.

Next he called his boss to inform him that he would be late.

"How are you, Joe?"

"Not too good. I'm not sure what time I'll be in. I found a dead body here in town. I'm waiting for a deputy to get here."

"Do you need to take the day off?"

"Nope, I need the money. I'll be in as soon as I can."

***

The dispatcher called Detective Sanders first, "I already dispatched a patrol car, but we have a dead body on Main Street. I don't know any more info than that. I still have to call the sheriff."

"I was getting ready to head out, anyway. My shift starts soon," Jordan replied.

Jordan turned to Agent Hamilton and explained, "We have a dead body on Main Street. There are no details at this time."

"I'll go ahead and follow you in."

It took them all of five minutes to get there. Deputy Andrews was already cordoning off the area.

"I was getting ready to call you," informed Deputy Andrews. "I haven't checked the body yet. I was waiting for the crime scene techs and coroner to get here. It appears to be the same guy. It's bad too, really bad."

A wave of nausea hit her as she looked at the body. Jordan pulled out her phone and quickly placed a call, "Sheriff, he struck again. The body is on Main Street under a gas lamp. Andrews has already called the team out."

"I'm on my way. The dispatcher had already called. I'll be pulling up any minute."

Jordan looked over at Agent Hamilton. "Any first impressions?"

"He is definitely losing control. It shows in the mutilations of the bodies and he's shortening the time between kills.”

They both stopped as the coroner pulled up along with the crime scene techs. After taking an initial look over the body, the coroner came over to them. “She’s still warm. She hasn’t been dead long. This one reeks of alcohol, so I’ll run a blood alcohol on her. He didn’t keep this body long. Unlike the other bodies he didn’t care if the wounds killed; these are deeper than those on the previous victims. He cleaned the body thoroughly again with bleach and acid. However, this time he even douched her with acid. I have to wait for labs for any definite answers. I do think she was too drunk to realize what was happening to her.”

“It’s too bad we don’t have a picture of her to pass around to the local bars,” Jordan speculated.

“I have a feeling that prior to death she was beautiful. He seems to go for the pretty young girls,” Detective Johnson stated. Jordan jumped slightly when she realized that both he and the sheriff were standing behind her. They must have shown up while the coroner was speaking.

“Let’s take this to the office everyone. That way we can get some fresh coffee, and look at this with new eyes,” Agent Hamilton explained.

***

Agent Hamilton looked over the information they had so far. As everyone gathered around the conference room, he stated, “Whoever committed these murders is a true piece of work. The ways the bodies are displayed confirm that the killer is extremely proud of his work. He is definitely showing off."

Jordan pondered out loud, "Is it the thrill of the hunt or the actual kill that excites this killer?"

"It is more than likely a combination of the two, unfortunately. He sees this as a game."

Sheriff Matthews said, "This town has never seen a serial killer, especially one like this sociopath. No one knows what to think of this."

"Well, he shows true pride in his showmanship. It's as if the torture itself is his motivation. I'm willing to bet there are bodies that he just never put on display. He has suddenly found the need to tell us that he has been living here, doing this right under your noses and you never knew until now. He is sending you a message, and he truly savors every moment of it. Hell, he may actually enjoy tormenting us with the fact that he can do this right under our noses."

Murder Board

Victim

Sarah Metzger
DM – October 2
DOD – October 3
Carpet fibers from possible Ford van

Marilyn Hennessey
DM – November 3
DOD – November 5
No trace evidence found on/near body

Andrea Smith
DM – November 20
DOD – November 23
Trace amount of semen found on the body

Whitney Guillory
DM – December 5
DOD – December 8

Danielle Taylor
DM – December 15
DOD – December 16

Erica Singley
DM - December 21
DOD – December23

Jane Doe
DM - UKN
DOD – Jan 2

Location

Undetermined
Secluded
Isolated
Possible hunting camp ????

Unsub

Mid 30's
Possibly drives Ford van, possibly white in color
Caucasian
6 feet, plus ?
Well-built
In shape
Financially well off or unemployed
Sexual dysfunction

Personality

Cunning
Superiority complex

Method of Killing

Torture
Rape/sexual assault: pre and post mortem
Breast mutilation
Cleaning body after death with bleach and acid

Chapter 50

Mindy saw the note right away and rushed back to the conference room. "Jordan, it appears that you have another note."

Jordan inspected the envelope. Once again, no return address and postmarked Springport. He was smart enough to use the self-adhesive stamps and envelopes too. He was careful to make sure no *faux pas* was made.

"She enjoyed becoming my latest masterpiece."
Signed
The Hunter

Sheriff Matthews looked over at Jordan, "I can't believe he honestly thinks this poor girl enjoyed being tortured? He truly is demented then."

"I can't figure out what he thinks but I wouldn't call him demented. He is Satan reincarnated."

Chapter 51

Jordan knew that it would help her career immensely if she captured this demonic killer. Yet, she had no desire to be some kind of rogue cop. She wanted to achieve her success through good detective work. Everybody had to get along and play nice, especially since they were working hand in hand with the state troopers and the FBI. However, she wanted to be the one to slap the cuffs on this guy, and show the others that small town police were just as smart as the FBI and State Troopers, if not smarter.

When her phone started ringing, she looked down and saw it was the Sheriff's Office. "Sanders. What's up?"

Mindy was all excited, "As long as you have been here, this is the first time you have ever received flowers. I had to let you know."

Jordan smiled through the phone, and said, "Thanks for calling Mindy. I'll be in in a few to pick them up."

She hung up the phone and looked over at Alex. "Why did you send flowers to the office? What were you thinking?"

"Thanks for the compliment, but it wasn't me. When did I have the time anyway?"

"So, if it wasn't you then who would send me flowers? It's not like I have a bunch of men following behind me."

"I can think of one that is. Maybe we just got lucky."

"Who are you talking about?" After she asked the question, she knew exactly who he was thinking of.

She quickly called Mindy back. "I'm heading over right now. I need you to call the crime scene techs and have them meet me over there."

"For flowers? Why? They are so pretty."

"They may be from him."

"Oh. Oh no!"

"Don't touch anything until we get there."

Jordan and Alex quickly headed to the office, in hopes that they would finally get some of the evidence that they needed.

Mindy had left the flowers were she had put them, front and center on Jordan's desk. Jordan quickly rushed over to check them out.

The card on the flowers was signed "Until we meet in person". His intention may have been to scare her, but instead he just infuriated her even more.

Chapter 52

Sheriff Matthews woke up with a startle and drenched in a cold sweat. He had the recurring nightmare again. He kept dreaming that he was in a field of corpses and mutilated bodies.

In the dream, a faceless phantom was laughing a chilling laugh in the background. But he would never show himself though.

Sheriff Matthews couldn't imagine what these poor women had to endure before death. The pain had to be horrendous.

He sat up and tried to forget. He watched his wife sleeping beside him. That seemed to help relax him.

It was time to retire and spend more time with her. Right now they only saw each other when she came to help answer the phones at the sheriff's office.

He was more than ready to trade in his gun for a fishing rod. He would love to spend his days fishing on the bayou and spoiling his new grandbaby that would be here soon.

The Hunter was getting agitated. The press had yet to give his masterpieces the true coverage they deserved.

A sinister smile made its way across his face at the wonderful memories but he needed to hunt again. The anticipation was too great he couldn't wait any longer. He dressed all in black, to meld into the night, for this hunting trip. He grew hard just thinking about what was to come.

Tonight had to be perfect. He even had candles placed around the room to celebrate Valentine's Day. The hot wax would be the perfect turn on. Plus the way the candlelight flickered in the mirrors helped to create a romantic ambience. It should have her begging for more.

His blood rushed through his veins with exhilaration. His muscles tensed with excitement and the impending capture of his next prey. He could not wait to bring her back to his lair.

He was on an adrenaline high. He had a stun gun in one pocket and chloroform in the other. Either one would be perfect for the abduction; silent, and neither were deadly.

The perfect time to hunt was here. The sunlight faded away and night set in. When the earth was still and all was quiet. Something ominous, mysterious, filled with evil exuded from him. Malevolence surrounded him, churning the air around him. The darkness of the night brought life to the pure evil of his soul.

The night air was heavy with the scent of magnolia trees in bloom. The full moon helped to illuminate the walkway where the street lights missed.

***

Jessica Livingston recently began her new job with Channel 10. This story would be her first big break. She was tired of being a gopher. She was bound and determined to dig up some information on the elusive serial killer hunting women in and around Hope, Louisiana. Jessica wanted to visit the disposal locations at night to see what the killer saw.

She had been to the other locations already on previous nights, but tonight she was going to stop at the final one on her list, the Community Center. So far, she hadn't been able to find any new clues that the police had missed, but she was hopeful that something here was going to help her solve the case.

 She was focused on the Center; she didn't hear anyone come up behind her.

***

She was starting to wake up. As she fought hard against the restraints, she could hear her captor laugh at her struggles. Her body convulsed when he shocked her with a stun gun.

She felt chilled and groggy as her eyes fluttered open.

Due to her distorted vision, she could barely make out shapes. Everything was in black and white. She blinked repeatedly to get everything into focus. It took a while for her eyes to adjust. When she looked around, she saw that the room was mirrored floor to ceiling.

She suddenly became aware of the cool air hitting her naked body.

She was strapped to some kind of weird contraption and couldn't move. She tried to pull on the restraints, but they refused to budge. Heartbreaking sobs wracked her body as tears streaked down her cheeks.

As she heard the footsteps, she began to say the Our Father in her head. She never considered herself a religious person. She didn't go to church regularly. She did believe in God though, and the power of prayer. Lord help her, she knew the serial killer had abducted her.

The stories were true; there was a bogeyman. He only came out at night and he had her. She finally got her big break and would not live to tell her story.

Time seemed to move slowly and quickly at the same time. She couldn't keep track of what was happening to her, all she knew was pain.

She felt a searing hot pain rip through her body. She tried to force her eyes to close but he had glued them open. She couldn't even turn her head away from the horror. The mirrors showed her reflection from every direction. She was forced to watch over and over again as he stabbed her with the knife. He even raped her with the knife before he actually penetrated her. He never cut her deep enough to kill, just deep enough to bleed. No matter how hard she struggled, she couldn't break free.

He taunted her with a stun gun, "I just want to tease you with it, I won't knock you out. I want you to watch me play."

Her fate was sealed. She prayed for her life, prayed for mercy. But it seemed her desperate attempts to survive turned him on.

***

Her bravado was slipping. He finally broke her strong will. Like all the others, she started off with a defiant attitude, but he always broke them.

He could still feel her heartbeat lessening and see the life leaving her eyes. She didn't put up a fight at the end, just whimpered. Which pissed him off more. She should have fought all the way to the end, just as his *mon douce* Detective would have. His latest victim didn't even make it through the night. He didn't get to torture her the way he wanted to, the way he really wanted to torture the Detective.
His ears were listening to the sounds of the night, listening to make sure no one was coming. He could hear the bayou in the background and the wind blowing through the trees. The kill had left him exhilarated. Once he confirmed that he was alone, he

ventured to the local boat landing to pose her. He didn't want to hurry, everything had to be perfect.

Chapter 54

Troy Hebert ran his crab traps early this morning. They were nice sized and seemed to be full. Now he had to get them iced down and over to the house for his wife to sell while he cleaned up. She called earlier to tell him that people were already calling for crab. It would be a good day indeed.

As he headed in he noticed someone already sitting on the landing. Hopefully he could talk the person into helping him out. Fellow fishermen around here tended to be helpful. They all knew what it was like to go out by yourself.

As he approached the dock he realized this poor soul wouldn't be able to help anyone. He quickly called his cousin, Chad Williams, a local deputy.

Chad wondered why Troy would call him this early. *"Quoi ça dit, bougre*? What's happening, buddy?"

"Mon ami, I'm at the boat landing. It's bad. It looks like someone decided to *dechirer*, tear into pieces, this poor *sha bebe*. You need to send help out something quick."

"I am heading out that way now. Don't go anywhere. I'll call the sheriff and let him know."

***

Chad quickly called Sheriff Matthews. "We got a body

at the landing. My cousin, Troy Hebert, called me.
He's waiting for us to get there."

"I'll go ahead and call the crime scene techs. Why
don't you call Detective Sanders? We'll all meet up
there."

Chapter 55

Detective Johnson was annoyed. "I'm getting tired of adding names to this thing. How in the hell is this guy moving around like he's invisible?"

Jordan quickly added, "I'm just glad we were able to find out who this last victim was. Thankfully Jessica's boss had an idea of what she was doing. If he hadn't been worried, I don't think we would have known who she was with how bad the body was."

Sheriff Matthews said, "You're right that we did luck out with her. But I don't understand why he waited so long in between the kills this time."

Agent Hamilton added, "We may have narrowed his field with the curfew. Now that people are aware of him there aren't as many women venturing out, during the day or night. Hell, this may even be part of his game."

"Let's just hope that we are making it more difficult for him to kill and he will give up."

"This killer is very calculating. So far we have no fingerprints, no trace evidence, and what DNA we do have there has been no match in CODIS. Let's go over what we know about this killer: he is organized, leaves almost little to no trace evidence. He blends in, almost chameleon like. He is cunning, intelligent. He believes he is smarter than the law enforcement agencies. He has an isolated place to take the victims so that he can torture, rape and kill them. He is brazen as he kidnaps and disposes of the bodies."

Everyone turned and looked at the murder board, lost in their own thoughts.

Murder Board

Victim

Sarah Metzger
DM – October 2
DOD – October 3
Carpet fibers from possible Ford Van

Marilyn Hennessey
DM – November 3
DOD – November 5
No trace evidence found on/near body

Andrea Smith
DM – November 20
DOD – November 23
Trace amount of semen found on the body

Whitney Guillory
DM – December 5
DOD – December 8

Danielle Taylor
DM – December 15
DOD – December 16

Erica Singley
DM - December 21
DOD – December23

Jane Doe
DM - UNK
DOD – Jan 2

Jessica Livingston
DM - February 13
DOD February 14

Location

Undetermined
Secluded
Isolated
Possible hunting camp

Unsub

Mid 30's
Possibly drives Ford van, possibly white in color
Caucasian
6 feet, plus
Well-built
In shape
Financially well off or unemployed
Sexual dysfunction

Personality

Cunning
Superiority complex

Method of Killing

Torture
Rape/sexual assault: pre and post mortem

Breast mutilation
Cleaning body after death with bleach and acid

Chapter 56

As Jordan walked into the office, Mindy ran up to her. "Jordan, he seems to enjoy communicating with you. You have another note."

The note was the same as before, no return address and postmarked Springport.

"Well, let's see what the sick little pervert has to say this time."

Did you enjoy my Valentine's Day masterpiece?
Signed
The Hunter

Sheriff Matthews looked over at Jordan. "I wish he would give us a clue as to why he waited so long in between these last two murders."

"Let's just hope it is even longer before he kills again, or better yet, not at all."

Chapter 57

Sheriff Matthews and Agent Hamilton went over to Rosy's Diner to grab a quick bite to eat. This was the one place Alex would miss when it came time to leave. Well, here and Jordan's.

Thankfully everyone allowed them to be in peace as they looked over their menus. When the waitress came to take their orders, she said, "I brought you some lagniappe, a little something extra, *mon cher*." With a quick wink to Agent Hamilton, she sauntered away.

"My favorite, crab boullettes. They are out of this world."

"I'm thinking our waitress seems to like you," the sheriff said trying to cover his laugh.

"She's just being friendly. Besides, I have enough on my plate right now without that worry."

Laughing the sheriff said, "Yeah, I don't think you want to piss Jordan off. The only reason you didn't notice her is because your eyes seem to gravitate to Jordan when she walks into the room. I'm willing to bet you are madly in love."

"I don't know if it's love or not, but we do enjoy each other's company. I'm also learning there is one good thing about small towns, the pleasantry of people. They always want to help out in some way. Even in bad times they seem to pull together."

"I can't argue there. Small town living is the best as far as I'm concerned."

The waitress placed their entrees in front of them. As usual, the food was seasoned to perfection. "I know I may be a northerner, but I don't understand why some chefs feel the need to make the food so spicy that you can't enjoy it. I'm eyeing another favorite dish for dessert, sweet potato beignets."

"If you don't watch it you are going to gain 30 pounds while you are here."

"I may start to get a complex. Jordan mentioned the same thing the other day. Eating seems to be my stress reliever I guess."

"Well I'm glad that you have been able to stay on here these past few months. I'm sure you have been needed at other places, with how hard it was to get you here to begin with," the sheriff remarked.

"That's what my team is for; they are some of the best. I am just glad that I have only had to give advice over the phone, that way I can be here if anything does just happen to pop up."

"I know we are thankful for that. But let's eat before the food gets cold," the sheriff said as he picked up his fork.

Alex followed suit, all the while thinking about how

lucky he actually was.

Chapter 58

The Hunter couldn't take his mind off of Detective Sanders ever since he saw her picture in the paper. She kept intruding in his dreams. He dreamed of her face, with its aristocratic nose and her blue eyes. He wondered if her eyes would get stormy when she was confronted with sheer terror. Her hair was as dark as midnight, his favorite time of the day.

It had been so easy to find out where the detective lived. The Hunter loved small towns, people loved to gossip. He also found out that she had a boyfriend, the FBI profiler. The gossip around town was that they were inseparable. That could make capturing her a little riskier, but it added a new intrigue to the game.

She was such a seductive woman. Sleeping with Mr. FBI the first night he came to town. She fit in with the rest of the women, all whores. All meaningless sluts.

He found a perfect hiding spot to observe her while she was at home. He wasn't ready to let her know he knew where she lived. That wouldn't fit into his plans for her. He had to be well prepared. This prey would be a bigger adversary than he originally planned. When he made his move she had to be unarmed and alone. Her guard would be down at home. Surely Mr. FBI wasn't there all the time. He couldn't afford to have any witnesses.

After she left for work, he would sneak into her house. He had to gather as much information about her as he could.

From his hiding spot, he watched as she left for work, with her boyfriend right behind her. Her boyfriend spent the night again. The rumors around town really were true, she was banging the FBI guy. He wondered how Mr. FBI would feel when he discovered that even he couldn't protect her.

He carefully popped the lock to the back door. The locks in older houses were easy to jimmy. It surprised him that she lived in such a small house. The Hideaway was far bigger and even it would be considered on the small side. The aroma from the coffee still lingered in the kitchen.

As he walked through the house, he found that she was a messy little girl. They didn't even bother to make up the bed. The bedroom still smelled of sex, her perfume, and Mr. FBI's cologne. From the looks of things, he slept over quite often.   This presented a problem that he would have to rectify. He considered leaving a note on her pillow. However, she would be on guard if she knew he had visited her house.

The intrigue, or complete and utter fascination, he had with Detective Sanders was insane. If he wasn't careful, his obsession with her would be his undoing. He couldn't understand this intense fascination he had with her. Getting this close to her was a mistake, but he found he had no control over himself when it came to her. That would soon change, though. Soon he would prove to her he was in complete control of her.

The Hunter couldn't wait to torture her. His body

ached for her; he wanted to feel the life slipping from her body. His skin grew hot with anticipation. The need to kill her was a burning fire inside of him. He had to find another prey to kill and soon. That would help curb the hunger to kill Detective Sanders for just a while longer, he hoped.

Chapter 59

Maybe it was because of the gloomy night that had her guard up. Plus work had been chaotic, and her nerves were shot. Jordan honestly couldn't blame people, it was human nature to be leery, but they have had more people call in with accusations of possible suspects, neighbors up all hours of the night, and such. Every unknown noise caused a call into dispatch. The available personnel for just the day to day job responsibilities were being worked extensively. Plus, on top of everything else, they decided to increase patrols day and night. Hopefully it made it almost impossible for the serial killer to abduct a victim or at least they would catch him in the process. Thankfully the state troopers and FBI had been able to help out a great deal by offering surveillance.

The DJ on the radio was talking about the serial killer that Hope had and asking the public's opinion. This didn't help her calm down either. She flipped through the radio stations, hoping to find some music to listen to. She had to shake herself out of this mood. All she managed to do was scare herself silly. She couldn't wait for this day to be over so she could just soak in a hot bath and enjoy the quiet of her home.

***

As Jordan finally arrived home, The Hunter noticed how beautiful *mon douce* Detective was. Her stance gave the impression of a headstrong woman. He couldn't wait to break her spirit and take her beauty away from her. Why do women prize their beauty above all else? Surely they should care more about their children than their beauty.

He must not forget that she was a whore. All women were whores. No sooner than the FBI profiler arrived in town, she spread her legs wide open for him.

He could see her perfectly from his hiding spot. Unlike the other cops, she took care of her body. She had an athletic build to her. Her breasts did not seem to match her body type. Possible boob job? Could she also be that vain?

He couldn't help but languish over her breasts. They would make a marvelous addition to his collection.

He watched her ease into the bathtub and the bubbles swirled around her body. He couldn't wait to explore her body and taste those beautiful breasts. Right now it was time for him to leave *mon douce* Detective, soon very soon though they would meet. For now, he felt like hunting.

"Soon, my sweet Detective we shall meet."

He was enjoying tormenting her right now. Soon this little game he started would be coming to an end. The Detective would meet The Hunter.

Chapter 60

As much as he had enjoyed his new art project, The Hunter was considering doubling his kills. What would it be like to capture two at the same time and have them watch as he tortured the other? He already had difficulty in keeping an erection all night with one prey. Just the thought of two at once brought a rush of anticipation through his body. Just thinking about the masterpiece it would create sent a chill of exhilaration down his spine.

He immediately began to plot his next course of action. Maybe he could find friends out having fun together. But where to go hunting? Then it hit him, there was a bar just out of town. No one would think twice about someone helping two women to their car. Yes, that may actually work.

***

These were the type of nights he enjoyed, when the night sky matched his soul, black. He blended in. A sense of foreboding pulsed with life in the air around him. The moon and stars sensed his presence and went into hiding. Even the night creatures were silent, sensing the danger that lurked about.

The anticipation of the hunt pumped adrenaline through his veins. His mind and body were ready. He had been letting several weeks lapse between hunts to throw off the mindless law enforcement agencies working the case. It kept them guessing his next move.

It was time to hunt again. He waited until the need completely overcame him.

He saw the friends sitting together at the end of the bar. They didn't look old enough to be in here. They more than likely had fake ids. The bartender most probably didn't care. After all, money was money.

One of the girls wore a tight pair of blue jeans that made her derriere look really good. Her tank top was clearly a few sizes too small since her ample breasts spilled out of the thing.

Her friend wore a tight little mini skirt and crop sweater. Neither wore outfits that left much to the imagination about their bodies. The Hunter planned to purchase them a couple more rounds and persuade them to let him get them to their car. Better yet, he would offer to drive them home. He drove his dad's Corvette tonight. It may be showy, but no woman would trust a man driving a van to a bar.

***

Amber Comeaux and Nicky Bryant both attended Southern Louisiana State. They were unlikely friends, but hit it off after being assigned to the same dorm room.

Amber dreamed of being a fashion designer. Clothes were her passion. Well, that and partying. She wasn't ready to grow up just yet. That may be why she and Nicky became such good friends. Nicky kept her grounded.

Nicky hadn't decided just yet what she wanted to do with her life. She was leaning toward becoming a pharmacist. She wanted to be practical and choose a career that would always be in high demand. She sometimes feared that she was too grounded, which was why she let Amber talk her into going out tonight. Maybe she should let her hair down and have some fun.

***

"Come on, let's wake up. I'm ready to play."

Amber's head throbbed. She struggled to open her eyes. What happened? She felt as if she was drugged.

Once her eyes opened, sheer terror took over. She looked around and saw she was shackled naked to a wall. She noticed that Nicky was in a chair in the middle of the room with a table near it. There were crude medical instruments on the table. A shiver of fear rippled through her body as the scent of bleach overpowered her senses. The room smelled worse than a hospital.

Whatever the creep used to drug Amber with made her mouth extremely dry. Her father constantly reminded her that she was his rebellious child. Well, she was determined to fight now. Nicky already showed signs of despair, so she tried to offer words of encouragement; begged her to fight and to stop acting so helpless.

Frustrated, Nicky exclaimed, "We wouldn't be in this mess if you hadn't wanted to go out! Why do I always have to listen to you? Now do you see where it has gotten us?"

Every word Nicky said was true. "I was only trying to get you to loosen up and have some fun. You can be such a stick in the mud at times."

"Oh yeah, we are having some fun now. We are being held prisoner with no idea where we are even at. We are trapped in this room. The only way out is through that door, and I'm pretty sure it locks from the other side. That is, if we can possibly manage to get out of these damned restraints."

Amber remembered playing darts with a guy and him buying them drinks. She felt confident that Nicky was ok to drive, besides neither girl had wanted to accept a ride from a stranger in a bar. Even if he did have a cool looking car.

Amber had bet Nicky that they could get in a bar without being carded. Surprisingly, the bartender had even served them drinks. It was their freshman year of college and Amber wanted to have some fun. She kept telling Nicky she needed to loosen up and have some fun. Nicky was all study and no play.

Amber never realized they could end up in this much trouble. She should have listened to her parents more.

* * *

Once done, he left Amber bloody and weak. She tried to block out Nicky's screams as the bastard tortured her next. Amber tried to stay quiet, not to let out even a moan. She didn't want to give him the satisfaction of knowing she hurt. She attempted to look away as he attacked Nicky, but the mirrors made it impossible.

Amber desperately wanted to stay strong, but she felt her resolve wavering. Their captor took extreme pleasure in inflicting pain. She could tell from his arousal that he truly enjoyed this. She feared they would be raped before this ordeal was over.

"Nicky, please you must fight. Don't surrender."

He kept taking turns with the girls. While they were both alive, he didn't want to sew their mouths shut. The other girl's screams would help to frighten the other. When one was at the point of passing out, he would stop and move to the next one.

Nicky's screaming was the worst. Amber desperately wished her eardrums would burst so she couldn't hear anymore.

When the killer looked towards her, Amber saw his true being. His eyes were empty, like his heart and soul. She cringed at the sight of Nicky's blood dripping off of his body.

Nicky let out the most horrific sounds. Amber watched with terror as he poured acid down her throat. He informed Nicky that he'd had enough of her screaming;

it was becoming a distraction to him. Even after
silencing her with the acid, he proceeded to glue and
stitch Nicky's mouth shut.

He turned to Amber and told her she would be next.
She was thankful at first when he didn't grab the acid.
He did, however, take the pliers and pull out her teeth,
before proceeding.

"Now," he said, "I don't have to listen to your friend's
screaming and your smart ass mouth."

Looking over at Nicky, Amber knew he didn't need to
silence her. Nicky was dead, if not she was close to it.
She cried for her friend and prayed that her own
"punishment" wasn't the same as Nicky's torture.

As Amber looked at Nicky's mutilated body slumped in
the shackles, an overwhelming sense of helplessness
consumed her. This was all her fault. If only she hadn't
insisted they go out and party. She felt broken. She
tried to fight back the nausea rising in her throat. She
couldn't help but stare at what remained of poor
Nicky's tattered body.

Amber felt weak, faint. She couldn't endure anymore.
Even though she couldn't scream out loud, her
screams echoed in her mind. She was ready to beg for
death, if only she could.

***

The night air was still cool, even if the days were
warming up. His blood flowed like molten lava through

his veins. Maybe the night air would help cool his skin flushed from the excitement of the kill. The scent of blood lingered in his nostrils, helping to keep his adrenaline pumping.

The Hunter still had his parents' home in the city, but he preferred the cabin. Here he felt at ease , he could be himself. He didn't have to worry about those nosy neighbors like he did in the city.

He carefully loaded the girls up in the pirogue and headed into town. It would be only fitting for the two friends to go to the playground.

***

Deputy Andrews decided to make one final patrol of downtown before shift change. On his way back to the office, he saw something in the newly constructed playground area over at the Community Center.

This was the first time he had felt faint since the bodies started being displayed. He called Detective Sanders at once.

"We have two bodies over at the Community Center playground.   This killer is seriously demented."

"Wait, did you say two bodies?" He could hear the confusion in her voice as she asked.

"*Oui.* I've never seen anything like it. They are almost entwined on the slide. I don't think I'll ever let my kids play here again. That image will be permanently fixed into my mind."

"I'm on my way. Does Sheriff Matthews know?"

"No, I called you first."

"Please inform him. I'll call Johnson on my way into town and pick him up. It is going to be a very long morning."

***

Looking at the bodies, she knew the coroner would have his work cut out for him today.

The coroner came up to Jordan a while later. "We are getting ready to transport the bodies. The mutilation was worse this time. It appears that he used more acid than he has in the past. Unfortunately, it will take me a while to untangle the bodies. He did quite a number on them."

"Thanks doc."

"You know, I've seen some bad things in my line of work but this one takes the cake."

Chapter 61

Johnson was confused, "A double murder. What the hell? One isn't enough? "

Agent Hamilton knew the unsub was getting bolder. He wanted to prove, at least in his mind, that he was smarter than all of them with his abductions and disposals in high risk locations.

All the women were beautiful. So far that was the physical characteristic the women had in common.

Alex addressed the group. "The unsub is attempting to take away the physical beauty from these women. The rape is meant to degrade and humiliate them, but the torture is his ultimate goal."

Shaking his head, he continued, "The thrill of the hunt is starting to wear off faster. He's escalating and showing a loss of control in the torture of his prey. This may soon lead to his capture.

"Somewhere along the way, possibly in his childhood, someone made him feel worthless. Possibly his mother. Maybe she put her beauty before her love for him. Now he is trying to get your attention and prove that he is not worthless. He has an attitude that says look at me; I've outsmarted all of you.

"As far as his notes to Detective Sanders, he wants to make sure that she knows he has her in his sights. He's injecting himself into the investigation without drawing too much attention to his actual identity. He's getting a charge letting her know she has no idea who he is. He is seeking power and control through foremost fear, then torture, rape and ultimately death."

Victim

Sarah Metzger
DM – October 2
DOD – October 3
Carpet fibers from possible Ford Van

Marilyn Hennessey
DM – November 3
DOD – November 5
No trace evidence found on/near body

Andrea Smith
DM – November 20
DOD – November 23
Trace amount of semen found on body

Whitney Guillory
DM – December 5
DOD – December 8

Danielle Taylor
DM – December 15
DOD – December 16

Erica Singley
DM = December 21
DOD – December23

Jane Doe
DM - UKN
DOD – Jan 2

Jessica Livingston
DM - February 13
DOD February 14

Jane Doe 2 and Jane Doe 3DM - February 21
DOD February 23

Location

Undetermined
Secluded
Isolated
Possible hunting camp

Unsub

Mid 30's
Possibly drives Ford van, possibly white in color
Caucasian
6 feet, plus
Well-built
In shape
Financially well off or unemployed
Sexual dysfunction

Personality

Cunning
Superiority complex

Method of Killing

Torture

Rape/sexual assault: pre and post mortem
Breast mutilation
Cleaning body after death with bleach and acid

Chapter 62

Mindy had started to dread the mail now. Especially since those notes started arriving. Her day seemed to get worse when she saw another note, this time on top of the morning's mail.

"Jordan, you have another note."

Jordan exclaimed, "This guy is getting on my last nerve."

They were weak.
Signed,
The Hunter

***

This killer has to be caught. Jordan suspected that the killer was watching her, waiting for a perfect moment to strike. She would never admit it out loud, but she feared one day soon he may sneak up on her, catch her off guard. She was just being paranoid, letting her imagination run wild. However, he had managed to sneak by all of them in the past.

She had to stop thinking like this; it wasn't doing anybody any good. Between all of them, they would figure out who he was. They were smarter than him. He had just gotten lucky so far but his luck had to run out soon.

Chapter 63

The patrons remembered the two girls being at the bar for a bit, but didn't remember seeing them leave. After more questioning, the bartender recalled serving them drinks and that a guy had also bought them some. Unfortunately, the guy wore a ball cap pulled down low on his head so the bartender couldn't make out his face. This was also the type of bar where id's weren't needed, just cold hard cash.

No one that they questioned remembered seeing a white utility van in the parking lot. This was the type of place where it would have stuck out too.

Again, too many unanswered questions. Did he drive another vehicle? Was this their guy or did they have to worry about a copycat? Or did this killer have a collection of cars at his disposal? Was that why he went undetected?

"You're kidding me right? With that many witnesses, how is it possible no one saw anything? This has to be some kind of cruel joke. " Sheriff Matthews said as he leaned back in his chair.

"I wish it was. They all had the same story; no one saw a thing at the bar that night. It was a cash only bar, no credit cards. Deposits are made every night; no cash was left on the premises. The bank processed the deposits first thing this morning. The cash has already been sorted through so there is no chance of fingerprinting any of it. The only reason that we even know their names, Amber Comeaux and Nicky Bryant, is because the bartender thought they were cute and wrote them down."

Sheriff Matthews stared at Jordan in complete disbelief. "Come on, how does this guy go completely unnoticed?"

"I guess he blends in with all the other rednecks. He had to have scoped out the place beforehand or he knows the bar. The guy that bought drinks for the girls wore a baseball cap. No one remembers anything distinguishing about him, just that he fit in with the crowd there."

"Of all the rotten luck. Well, you might as well look at the lab reports while you are here." Sheriff Matthews handed the lab reports over to her.

"Even after killing two poor women at the same time, he's careful not to leave any evidence. And then just in case he does leave evidence or semen behind he makes sure he douches them with acid. How are we supposed to catch this guy if he can start to escalate with no mistakes?" Jordan asked, not expecting an answer.

Chapter 64

This was the first morning in a while that Sheriff Matthews could enjoy a sunrise with his wife. They were sitting on the porch sipping hot tea. With the weather switching from cold to hot during the days and being so run down from work, he felt a cold coming on. His wife, whom he loved very much, felt he didn't need his coffee this morning but hot green tea with honey instead.

He hated to admit it, but Mindy had been right. His scratchy throat was already starting to feel better. However, he couldn't wait to get to the office and pour himself a cup of strong coffee. He still wasn't sleeping at night and needed a serious caffeine fix.

By the time he made it home that night he knew he had the flu or at least a really bad virus. His throat was raw and he was running a fever. Mindy took one look at him and sent him off to bed. She brought him a hot toddy soon after to help.

"You need to take better care of yourself."

He looked at his wife and complained with a tired sigh, "I can't afford to be sick with this case going on right now."

Chapter 65

They all walked into the Sheriff's Office to find another rose bouquet waiting for Jordan.

I know you will be better
From
The Hunter

Sheriff Matthews was exasperated with the case. "He is playing us like fools. I have a meeting at the mayor's office. He wants to be caught up on the case."

As the sheriff walked over to the mayor's office, he felt as if he was letting the whole town down every time another murder took place. What made it worse was that the unsub was toying with one of his deputies. Playing a cat and mouse game with her that only he knew the rules to.

When he arrived at the Mayor's office, Frannie Gilbertson was at her desk, cheery as always. Mayors may come and go here, but Frannie had been the mayor's secretary for as long as he could remember. She talked about retiring and sitting at home, but no one in town believed her. She enjoyed being in the thick of things, knowing what was going on in town. If you wanted to know what was happening, all you had to do was ask Frannie.

"Good morning Sheriff. How are you feeling today? Better I hope? Mindy mentioned you have a touch of the flu."

"I'm feeling better, thank you. I have a really fine nurse taking care of me. This weather sure isn't helping any of us."

"No, it isn't. Mother Nature needs to decide if it's going to stay warm or cold. I never know if I should leave the heat or air conditioning on when I leave for work. I'm not too happy about having to run my air conditioner right now, but then again I'm not too fond of the cold either."

"Is the Mayor in this morning?"

"He is, and he is expecting you. Why don't you go on back? I'll bring you both some coffee and cinnamon rolls. I made them both fresh."

Sheriff Matthews knocked on the Mayor's door before entering.

"Sheriff, I was just wondering how you were doing."

"Fine, fine," Sheriff answered.

"Good. What about the deputies? Are they holding up okay with all these murders going on? I'm worried about them. This isn't something they typically handle."

"The deputies are holding up fine. However, we may need a little extra manpower if we want to catch this guy. The killer has stepped up his taunting of Detective Sanders."

"I'm trying to get us more manpower. I've been talking to other town mayors to see if they can lend a hand or at least help bump up patrols along parish and town lines. Everyone seems to be feeling the economic crunch.

"I'm stressing how bad we need to catch this guy. He's not just hunting girls here; he's also abducting women from other areas. I reminded them that even though the dead bodies have been found here, it didn't mean the killer couldn't, or wouldn't, change locations to dispose of the bodies."

"I appreciate that. Maybe we should also invite the local sheriffs and mayors to one of our morning pow wows. Let them witness firsthand what we are dealing with. We need to stress the importance of not divulging information to the press. Everything needs to stay contained within the walls of the conference room."

"I like that idea. I'll get to work on that today. As soon as I get confirmation, I'll give you a call."

Chapter 66

From the outside, the town looked ready to celebrate the upcoming festivities. Even the stores along Main Street had decorated their window fronts for Mardi Gras.

Truth was no one in the town was in a festive mood. They knew something sinister was lurking about here. A killer possibly lived among them, bringing a sense of despair to the town.

That knowledge alone tainted the upcoming festivities. Hope was all about tradition though and traditions must be upheld. It would be a long time however before life would be back to normal here.

An uneasy feeling came over Jordan; almost a sixth sense that she was being watched. This wasn't the first time she had felt like this. She slowly turned around but didn't see anything.

***

The Hunter stepped deeper into the brush. He wanted to check on his sweet Detective before heading off.

"Mon cher, you will meet me soon. Until then, I have others to hunt." The Hunter whispered into the breeze to *mon douce* Detective.

The Hunter believed none of these bitches deserved to live. Women were worthless whores. They cared about their beauty and how to spend money that day, nothing else. Women were just plain deceitful and untrustworthy. They needed to be treated like the dogs they were. After all, his mom took beatings for years without saying anything. All she cared about was that afterwards his dad would give her some spending money to make up for the bruises and humiliation.

Women lie to you, would tell you whatever you wanted to hear. His mom made plenty of empty promises to both him and his dad.

A woman's beauty was superficial, on the inside their true ugliness lived. The Hunter harbored a deep hatred for women in general. He allowed the darkness of that hatred to take over his soul.

These women were his artistic masterpieces. The true beauty he saw in them became preserved forever.

Chapter 67

The Hunter noticed cars parked up and down the street. This might be the perfect place to hunt tonight. He found a good hiding place and staked out the area. It looked to be a Mardi Gras party in full swing. He wasn't sure if he would be bringing home two prey, but he would take at least one trophy home.

He made himself comfortable and waited. A couple of hours later he saw the perfect prey. A couple of women giggling like a bunch of schoolgirls leaving the party. They stumbled down the road, not paying any attention to their surroundings. What luck, they were walking to where he had hidden the van. He was glad he had decided to drive the van tonight. Nobody paid attention to utility vans anymore. He would have to act fast to stun both girls. *What a treat.*

***

Kat was shivering. She couldn't seem to wake up. She felt sluggish and had trouble moving. Uneasiness began to settle over her body. She tried hard to clear her mind. When her eyes finally focused in on an image, she saw herself in the mirror's reflection, but she didn't recognize the person looking back at her. She couldn't believe that that image was actually her.

She was confused and her head was throbbing. She knew she'd had a lot to drink, but not enough to cause this massive of a hangover.

It was all coming back to her in bits and pieces. The fog started to lift from her mind. She remembered being at the Mardi Gras party at Gina Collins' house. She and Diane had ridden together since they both lived in Banbridge now. Whereas Gina had decided to stay in Hope and marry her high school sweetheart. There were so many cars at Gina's party that they had to park quite a ways down the road. They had way too much fun reuniting with everyone. She couldn't believe that they turned thirty this year.

Kat started to wonder where Diane was when she heard a noise of some kind. It sounded almost like a whimper.

"Diane, is that you?"

"Kat, what's going on? Do you know where we are? I feel like I have a massive hangover. I don't remember drinking that much. I can't seem to get it together."

"I can't move my arms and legs. Can you?"

"Just barely."

Kat could hear something that sounded like chains rattling, and then jumped when she felt someone touch her. "Kat, I'm right here by you. We are side by side. We are restrained together on the floor. Please try to open your eyes. I think we are in serious trouble. We are both naked."

Kat finally opened her eyes and saw her surroundings. "I think I was better off not seeing. You're right, this doesn't look good."

"Kat, do you remember hearing the news reports about a serial killer?"

"I vaguely remember something about that. I'm not too sure though. Don't even think it; there is no way we were abducted by a serial killer. This is just a bad dream, a nightmare."

"Yeah, the exact same one. Snap out of it."

Sheer terror took over Kat's thoughts. They couldn't have been abducted by that guy. They were here for a Mardi Gras party, to have fun.

"We need to stop and think this through. Now is not the time to panic. We are both shackled to the floor. Is there something we can reach to get out of these blasted things?" Diane asked.

Kat looked around and saw the chair and other torture devices and tried not to concentrate on them.

"There is a table with some kind of instruments. They are closer to you. Can you move close enough to get something?" Diane asked her.

"Let me see." She struggled to move, but she didn't have much slack.

They both froze when they heard footsteps approaching and attempted to move in close together. The door opened and a naked man wearing only gloves entered the room. They turned to each other with terror in their eyes.

"I hope you're ready to begin?" asked their captor. "I've been waiting patiently for you to wake up. I have a new game I want to add to my regimen and you will be the first to try it out. I've rigged this little stick to shock you only enough to hurt you. If you refuse to do something or you don't do it to my liking, you will be shocked. I will give each of you a sample so that you know what to expect."

He gently touched one and then the other with the stick. It instantly sent a small, unpleasant current through their bodies.

"Now, that was on the lowest setting. I do have a setting control where I can turn up the levels higher. Would either of you like to see what that feels like ? "

They both vigorously shook their heads no. This man looked inhuman.

He informed them, "Don't worry girls, no one will be left out. You will each take turns."

***

He would beat and viciously rape one, then switch to the other. After all, he couldn't allow just one of them to have all the fun.

Both women had tears streaming down their faces by now. He quickly became tired of torture as it lost its thrill. He was ready to take it to the next level. Besides, the women had begun to tune out the pain he implemented.

"No! Please don't. You don't have to do this!" one of them screamed out.

This one was losing control; she couldn't find the strength to be strong, to fight. He continued to taunt her, "We can't have any of that now. It distracts me when you are too loud."

He proceeded to pull all of her teeth out. Once done, he glued and stitched her mouth shut.

Just when she looked ready to pass out from all the pain, he slapped her face and switched to her friend.

His menacing laughter sent chills down her spine. "Now it's your turn. I must be fair."

Chapter 68

Mardi Gras was a huge celebration in Louisiana. King Cakes went on sale not long after Christmas.

The local Krewes were having their Mardi Gras balls, planning their parade floats, and costumes for the events. Mardi Gras was one thing Sheriff Matthews could live without this year. Not only did it mean that summer would be here shortly, but the killer continued to taunt them. It had been over six months with no leads or suspects. With each crime scene you never knew what you would discover, except of course no evidence.

The floats were lined up in succession at the dock ready to go for the morning parade. A cop had been assigned to keep a close look out in case the murderer decided to dispose of a body here. No locals had been reported missing, but that didn't mean he hadn't abducted someone from somewhere else.

The town always had a boat parade along the bayou for the celebration. Most towns did theirs on the main roads, which was one of the reasons Hope's was even more popular. It was something different, unique. It was as if the threat of the serial killer lurking about hadn't scared them off.

* * *

As The Hunter eased up to the floats, he saw the deputy and his Detective. Just as he suspected, they were watching the area. It was a risky challenge, his heart was racing. This was his chance to show Sheriff Matthews and his lackeys how smart he was. This was his chance to outwit them.

He contemplated taking *mon douce* Detective back home with him tonight when he saw her. But it was too dangerous. She wasn't worth the risk of getting caught.

Chapter 69

Sheriff Matthews swore that he heard a phone ringing in his dream.

Suddenly Mindy was shaking him awake. "John, you need to take this phone call."

"I thought I was dreaming."

"It's not a dream, it's the dispatcher."

"Sheriff here. Please don't tell me another body was found."

"No sir, it was two again. Detective Sanders asked that I give you a call. They don't know how he managed to get past them, but there were two bodies displayed on the King and Queen's Mardi Gras Float."

"Alright, I'll be heading in. I'm calling Hamilton now."

Sheriff quickly hung up the phone, and covered his face with his arm. "Mindy, we just can't seem to catch a break with this case."

Mindy jumped out of bed and replied, "Get dressed, I'll start the coffee. It's going to be a long day."

The Sheriff sighed as he dialed Hamilton. "We found two bodies this morning."

"I just got off the phone with Jordan. The coroner won't know for sure until an autopsy has been completed, but he is fairly certain that both women died around the same time. He definitely added some form of acid to his arsenal of torture techniques.

"I don't have to tell you that this isn't good. He is stepping up his game, getting riskier, and more dangerous. Killing one at a time is no longer giving him the sexual gratification he needs. Until he finds that release, he will continue to experiment. There is no telling how long this will appease him. We have to capture this guy. He has not made any mistakes yet and is being overly cautious. This is an extremely dangerous individual."

"I understand. Listen, tell everyone to meet in the conference room as soon as they can. I think it's time to look over this with completely fresh eyes."

Alex quickly agreed, "Sounds good. We will see you shortly."

***

Sheriff Matthews continuously paced the conference room. He was tired of seeing people he knew murdered by this bastard. Even in the depraved state that the killer had left the bodies in, he had recognized the victims as soon as he saw them. "No suspects, no leads, no evidence, nothing. There seems to be a trend here."

Detective Johnson offered, "All we are doing is adding more names to the murder board."

Mindy rushed into the room. "Jordan, you have another note."

Jordan just stared at the envelope and sighed, "I hate to open it."

Friends Till The End
Signed,
The Hunter

Murder Board

Victim

Sarah Metzger
DM – October 2
DOD – October 3
Carpet fibers from possible Ford Van

Marilyn Hennessey
DM – November 3
DOD – November 5
No trace evidence found on/near body

Andrea Smith
DM – November 20
DOD – November 23
Trace amount of semen found ON body

Whitney Guillory
DM – December 5

DOD – December 8

Danielle Taylor
DM – December 15
DOD – December 16

Erica Singley
DM - December 21
DOD – December23

Jane Doe
DM - UKN
DOD – Jan 2

Jessica Livingston
DM - February 13
DOD February 14

Amber Comeaux and Nicky Bryant
DM - February 21
DOD February 23

Jane Doe 2 and Jane Doe 3
DM - UKN
DOD March 2

Location

Undetermined
Secluded
Isolated
Possible hunting camp

Unsub

Mid 30's
Possibly drives Ford van, possibly white in color
Caucasian
6 feet, plus
Well-built
In shape
Financially well off or unemployed
Sexual dysfunction

Personality

Cunning
Superiority complex

Method of Killing

Torture
Rape/sexual assault: pre and post mortem
Breast mutilation
Cleaning body after death with bleach and acid

Chapter 70

The Hunter dressed in all black which allowed him to spy on his prey. Black melded into the night better than the camouflage. He slipped on his ski mask and was ready.

He secured the boat in a secluded area and walked where he needed to go. It was easier to travel by the bayou right now since the cops were busy patrolling the roads. He hiked through the woods, being as quiet as he could.

He was armed with both a gun and knife just in case someone did notice him. It would be a quick, silent kill. The gun was equipped with a silencer, although no one around here would jump at the sound of a gun going off. Someone was always hunting or shooting at something, but it would be better not to draw any unwanted attention.

He crept through the dense foggy night to his viewing spot. The air itself changed around The Hunter. It was as if it knew something evil, dark and deadly lurked in him. The wind picked up momentum with each step he took; rain weighed heavily in the gloomy clouds. The bad weather lingered around all day, as if waiting for him to make his move.

Not far from where his Detective was, The Hunter watched her at night. She headed straight for the bathtub when she made it home.

He couldn't wait to run his hands up and down her legs

and explore her body. He wanted to probe and tease her with one of his unique tools. He still wasn't sure which he would start with. He couldn't wait to get her on all fours and treat her like the bitch she was. He would ride her hard; punish her for being a whore. He wanted to watch her blood slowly oozing from her body and onto the floor.

The anticipation of the kill caused his heart to beat faster. He enjoyed stalking her and sending her little notes so she wouldn't forget he was always near. He couldn't wait to see the fear in her face when they finally met.

He was rock hard and throbbing now. He needed to find relief so he could think. While he watched her bathe, he stroked himself fast and hard.

***

A shiver ran through Jordan, even though the water in the tub was nice and hot. An eerie feeling snaked down her spine. It was as if she was being watched. She was being ridiculous, but she couldn't shake the feeling. She quickly dried herself off, put on some sweats, and stepped out onto the back porch to see if she noticed anything. A chill was still in the night air. Spring would be here soon, but winter wasn't ready to say its final farewell yet.

The night was quiet, almost too quiet. No noises came off the bayou. Looking around, Jordan didn't see anything out of the ordinary. As she headed back inside she still couldn't shake the feeling that she was being watched.

Alex met her at the door, "What's up?"

"Nothing, just a feeling I couldn't shake. Let's go back in."

***

The Hunter's mind was in overdrive right now. The FBI profiler was there again. He never seemed to stay away from her house. She was like a bitch in heat. The Hunter kept envisioning the capture of his prey. He had to get her away from the FBI profiler if he wanted to succeed. He would have to move quickly. If he closed his eyes, he could almost taste her blood on his lips. He was rock hard again. He would have to kill soon to satisfy his urges before it was *mon douce* Detective's turn.

Anticipation hummed its way through his body. He spent the whole night watching *mon douce* Detective sleeping with the FBI profiler. Soon, he would have the Detective and perform all of his darkest desires on her body.

Chapter 71

Sandy Ohr had to get out of the house for at least five minutes or she would go crazy. Everyone was home for Easter and it was just too many people under one roof. It was such a pretty day too, even if it was a little humid. She decided to take a walk along the bayou to get some fresh air and unwind. Maybe she would scope out where to hide the Easter eggs for the children.

Since the water was choppy, she knew better than to hide any eggs close to the banks. They would have to make sure the kids stayed away from the water.

She was starting to relax and enjoy her day. She could feel herself unwinding from the stress. All of a sudden goose bumps traveled up her arm, the hairs on her neck rose. It was as if someone was watching her.

***

The Hunter should head back home with daybreak here. As he left his hiding spot he heard a movement up ahead and moved deeper into the brush. He couldn't believe his luck; a woman was walking all by herself and she was headed right for him.

There was no sense in letting this opportunity pass him by. She was small enough that he could hide her in the boat.

He quietly made his way up behind her and covered her mouth before she could even let out a scream. She struggled hard against him, kicking and biting whatever part she could reach. As he started to drag her towards his boat, he didn't realize that she had lost one of her shoes.

****

Blood was already leaving streaks down her body. The pain was excruciating. The flesh on her ankle gaped open where he cut her tattoo away with great precision. She wasn't sure what this maniac wanted with her, but he was certifiable. She was certain she had been abducted by the killer Sheriff Matthews and Jordan had been talking about.

There were no windows in the room so she had no idea how long she had been here. He had offered her no food or water and was forced to relieve herself right where she lay.

She begged him, "Please stop. You're hurting me."

She felt powerless, weak. She despised not being in control over a situation.

"You're handling the torture so well though. Better than I ever imagined. I'm thinking of intensifying it to see how you handle more pain."

If only she could lash out at him. He would kill her, but she refused to go down without a fight. She would give it all she had left in her. She had never been a quitter.

With a maniacal laugh, he stated, "I love it when you fight. You can try all you want but no one has ever broken free. I designed these all myself and have used quite a few subjects to perfect my play room. Now, as much as I love hearing your voice, it's time to silence those screams."

Fear bubbled up inside of her. If she was afraid before, she was terrified now.

"No, no, no. You don't have to do that. I can be quiet. Please no."

He gave a menacing laugh, before he glued and stitched her mouth shut.
"Should we start with the knife or the prodder? I'm thinking the prodder first. It's so messy when the knife is used first and it can be difficult to clean the blood off of the prodder."

His eyes were empty, barren. No soul could be found, his heart must be cold as ice. The devil himself would be afraid of this man. He had created a true hell on earth. When he picked up the knife, she accepted her fate.

She felt the blade slice open her skin, the blood trickled down her body. The cuts weren't enough to kill, but caused a white, hot pain that could not be disregarded.

Death loomed over her, taunting her. She was ready to die.

***

The night was still, as if waiting for him to make his move. The Hunter considered himself to be one of the creatures of the night. After all, he did his best work at night.

The pirogue glided through the murky waters. The limbs of the weeping willows gracefully blew in the night wind. An ancient oak tree, at least a century old by now, grew in a bend of the bayou and Spanish moss hung from the gnarled branches. A low lying branch dripping with moss gave him the perfect cover to hide his pirogue so that he could display his masterpiece. He pulled the pirogue onto the bank and secured it to the tree. The stairs leading to the courthouse would be the perfect setting for his latest masterpiece.

Chapter 72

Sheriff Matthews had come to hate ringing phones. They never brought good news.

"Let me guess, we have another double homicide."

Startled, the dispatcher replied, "No sir, it is just one body. But sir, it looks like it might be Detective Sanders' neighbor. She asked that I let you know the crime scene techs are on their way. He posed the body on the steps of the courthouse."

"Great, another 'up yours' to us I'm guessing."

***

By the time they finished, no one was in the mood to talk. Jordan walked over to the murder board and grimly added yet another name.

Murder Board

Victim

Sarah Metzger
DM – October 2
DOD – October 3
Carpet fibers from possible Ford van

Marilyn Hennessey
DM – November 3
DOD – November 5
No trace evidence found on/near body

Andrea Smith
DM – November 20
DOD – November 23
Trace amount of semen found ON body

Whitney Guillory
DM – December 5
DOD – December 8

Danielle Taylor
DM – December 15
DOD – December 16

Erica Singley
DM – December 21
DOD – December23

Jane Doe
Last Seen December 31
DOD – Jan 2

Jessica Livingston
DM – February 13
DOD February 14

Amber Comeaux and Nicky Bryant
DM – February 21
DOD – February 23

Kathleen Landry and Diane Berkley
DM –February 28
DOD – March 2

Sandy Ohr
DM - UNK
DOD April 16

Location

Undetermined
Secluded
Isolated
Possible hunting camp

Unsub

Mid 30's
Possibly drives Ford van, possibly white in color
Caucasian
6 feet, plus
Well-built
In shape
Financially well off or unemployed
Sexual dysfunction

Personality

Cunning
Superiority complex

Method of Killing

Torture
Rape/sexual assault: pre and post mortem
Breast mutilation
Cleaning body after death with bleach and acid

Chapter 73

The news crews were already crawling all over the scene. A barricade had to be set up to keep them away from the crime scene, but they remained hovering over the area like vultures.

"Sheriff, do you have any clue as to who the serial killer is?"

"No comment."

"Sheriff, what are you doing to keep the public safe?"

"Again, no comment. A statement will be issued shortly."

Looking over at his deputies, the sheriff exclaimed, "Deputy Andrews, we need to make sure these news crews and bystanders stay back and out of the way. Feel free to arrest anyone that doesn't listen to you."

"Yes sir. It will be my pleasure."

Sheriff Matthews couldn't help but think of the mess this morning was turning out to be. Then, on top of it all, Jordan suspected that this psycho was watching her. A team was being arranged to stake out her house.

Until then, he wanted to check the area around her house just in case. The crime scene unit was still processing the area, so until they were done they couldn't do anything else.

"Sanders, Hamilton, why don't we slip over to your house and check things out. It'll be a while before they are finished up here and we can move in."

"Yes sir. That's fine with me."

***

The Hunter hid in the shadows, watching. He wanted to see his sweet Detective at work. He noticed the sheriff, Detective Sanders and the profiler leaving. Perhaps he should follow to see what would make them leave the crime scene. Could it be his sweet Detective just couldn't see her neighbor dead and had to leave?

They got in the sheriff's car and headed out. It would be difficult to follow the car without being noticed, but maybe if he was careful enough he could. Thankfully an overzealous news van also decided to follow the Sheriff.

As they turned down the road to where his Deputy lived, he knew this couldn't be good. He began to sweat as he wondered why they went to her house. No one would have witnessed him watching her. He was being careful. He pulled over a few streets down and walked along the bayou, hiding in the underbrush just to be extra careful.

His heart was pounding now. They were examining the perimeter of her yard. He hoped by some chance that they didn't find his hiding place. *Too late, they did.*

The FBI man called out for Sheriff Matthews and his Detective, "I think you'll need to take a look at this. It's hard to see her house clearly from here, but with the right equipment it can be done."

The Hunter didn't stay around to see what all they found. If they started to look further into the area, it wouldn't be wise for him to be here. He was starting to get nervous now; he didn't recall leaving anything in the area that could connect him. Just his footprints and he always made sure he wore different size shoes to keep his actual height and weight unknown.

***

"That son of a bitch. He's been watching me take a bath and God knows what else."

Jordan was fuming. She thought about all the times she had lingered in a hot bath; all the times she and Alex had sex. How much had this creep seen? How well did the blinds and curtains in her bedroom actually block out any possible peeping Toms? Since the bedroom overlooked the woods, how many times did she remember to close those same blinds and windows? She decided, come nightfall she would find out exactly how well you could see into her house.

"Let's have the FBI install surveillance cameras here in case he comes back."

Chapter 74

Jordan decided to go into the office a little late. She couldn't help but blame herself for Sandy's murder. They were never close friends, but they were neighbors. She was abducted not far from Jordan's house after all.

Her morning was interrupted when Mindy called her a little after 8:30 with bad news.

"You have another note."

"What does it say?" she asked.

Sighing Mindy replied, "I hate to open it."

"Please, just wait for the crime scene techs to open it and let me know what it says."

After a few minutes, Mindy replied, "I'm so sorry Jordan. It reads, *'Her masterpiece was no comparison to how great your masterpiece would be'*."

Chapter 75

The Hunter was proud of his latest handiwork. He just finished a new addition to his torture room. It reminded him of the stockades that were used decades ago. This would be perfect for holding the heads of his prey still while he worked on their eyes and pulled out their teeth. While the iron maiden worked well, he was getting bored with it. Besides, one could never have too many toys. He wanted more options readily available to keep it interesting.

Inflicting pain was the best way to show power and control. It was an addictive feeling; the best drug out there to him.

It was close to supper so he decided to go out and grab a bite to eat at Rosy's Diner. Maybe a good hunting spot would come to him while eating. It was hard to think on an empty stomach.

Rosy's Diner had a new waitress that caught his eye. He noticed her as soon as he walked in.

***

Becky Griffith was 34 years old and still hadn't figured out what she wanted to do. She knew she couldn't waitress for the rest of her life. She should do something more productive than partying in her spare time. She moved to Hope thinking she would finally grow up if she were away from the city. So far that hadn't happened. There were just as many places here to have a good time.

Becky noticed the stranger as soon he walked in the door. She motioned for him to sit at one of her tables. He was unconventionally handsome and it sure wouldn't hurt to at least flirt during dinner service. She and Randy broke up a month ago and she was getting desperate for some male companionship. Maybe he'd even offer to take her home.

Becky asked, "What can I get you handsome?"

The stranger asked, "What's good tonight?"

"You mean besides me?" *Oh lord, did I really say something that dumb. What a lame line, I must be desperate.* "The fried chicken is always good. If you want spicy, I recommend the crawfish etouffee."

"Spicy sounds good. I'll take the etouffee and a beer."

"Coming right at cha, cher."

They continued to flirt during the meal when he suddenly asked, "You new, mon cher? I don't think I've seen you here before."

"I've been here about a month or so. I usually work the day shift to leave my nights open. Martha asked me to switch with her so that she could spend some quality time with her husband and all. Whatever that means. Do you want any dessert?"

"You mean besides you?"

"Honey, I get off at ten o'clock if you are serious," she flirted right back.

"Well, I guess I'll have some coffee and something sweet, besides you for now, to kill time."

"Coming right up."

They continued to flirt back and forth until it was close to her quitting time.

"Look, cher, I need to run to the store before they close. I'll be back in time to pick you up. Don't worry."

"No problem. Um, I'm out of protection if you don't mind?"

Laughing he replied, "That's what I'm running to get. I wasn't prepared to meet someone at the restaurant."

"Seriously? Okay then. See you in a bit then?"

***

Renee Ellis had just started working at the local nursing home. It was an okay place to work, it paid what bills she had. Renee still lived with her parents but hopefully she would eventually save enough money to where she could move out soon. Living with her mom and dad put a cramp on the partying lifestyle.

Renee had just earned her LPN certificate and had decided to go for RN. That seemed to be where the money was. She still needed to work nights to pay for schooling. School wasn't cheap.

Renee was on her way home when her car died on her. *Great, just great. What a perfect way to end the night. My car dies in the middle of nowhere. There's no cell service out here either.*

Thankfully, civilization was in walking distance. She was also grateful the nursing home made them wear these god-awful ugly shoes. At least they were comfortable and you could walk in them.

***

The Hunter couldn't believe his luck. A car was broken down on the side of the road and a female figure headed his way. He may have time to abduct this one and still be back in time to get the other girl. He may be able to double his pleasure tonight, luck was on his side.

He pulled up to the side of the road, "Miss, you need some help?"

"Oh, thank you so much. My car just quit on me. I was going to call my dad to come and get me."

"I'm sorry I don't have a phone on me. Those things know your whole life and share it with the world."

"Well…"

He saw the doubt in her eyes. Before she could move away, he grabbed her head and hit it hard against the

SUV's door, managing to knock her out cold. He gagged, restrained her and tossed a blanket over her to hide her from Becky. She could sit up front, she was at least willing. If the need arose, he could easily stun her. Becky was so hot for him though that he didn't see the need until they were closer to The Hideaway.

He arrived at the restaurant with a few minutes to spare. He parked in the back and waited. Becky was the first one out. He was right; she was eager and ready to go. He flashed his lights at her and she came running.

"I was worried you had changed your mind."

"Nope. I've been thinking about all the things I'm going to do to you." Smirking to himself, she didn't know how true that was either.

"Well, let's go big boy. The night is young."

He groaned inwardly as she talked non-stop. He couldn't wait to shut her up. They were close to the turn off when his other captive started to move around and make noise.

"What's that? Do you have a dog in the back?"

Instead of answering her, he took out his stun gun and shocked her. *Peace and quiet at last*. He was in a hurry to get home, but couldn't afford to get stopped for speeding with two women in his SUV, especially when one was restrained and the other out cold.

When he reached the Hideaway, he carried Becky in first while she was still out. He restrained her in the chair and stripped her. The other one was next and he restrained her to a hook on the ceiling. After ensuring she was restrained just right, he reached for his knife and cut her clothes off her body.

The other girl was bassette, short. She would have to stand on her tiptoes to keep from causing her more pain. He could lower the restraints some, if he wanted to be nice. The restraints were on a pulley that could go up or down. However, he enjoyed watching her struggle.

What a delightful turn of events for him. Dinner, dessert, and a surprise all in a few hours. He couldn't wait to begin. However, it would be best if they fed off of each other's fear first. Eventually, he would have to close Becky's mouth. She was too much of a damned talker. He would have done it on the way here if he could have. These girls had to get each other in a sheer panic first. Psychological torture was first.

Becky started to groan. *Perfect, they were both waking up.*

****

Becky didn't even notice there was someone else in the room with her until she groaned. She was restrained in what reminded her of a stockade prison. It was a crude form of a stockade meant to keep the captive hunched over with their feet secured to a wall. Her head and arms were completely immobile. On top of that, she was naked.

Becky couldn't take her eyes from what was happening to the other girl, even if her eyes weren't glued open. She watched the torture as if in a trance. She was almost mesmerized by the girl being tortured beyond belief. This couldn't be real; it had to be a nightmare. The burning pain from her eyes being pried open remained a constant reminder of how real it was. The pain she was suffering, must be nothing compared to the pain this other woman was enduring right now. She feared her turn was fast approaching. It was obvious this wasn't the freak's first time. He enjoyed this way too much. The screaming and moaning didn't seem to bother him; in fact it appeared to be a turn on. More blood oozed from the girl's wounds, but he kept going.

However, he didn't want to kill her right away. She tried to twist and turn out of the bonds but to no avail. The screaming which had been piercing in the beginning was growing weaker. Blood slowly continued to pool at her feet. Both women had tears running down their faces.

* * *

The more the woman screamed from the whip striking her bare skin the more he laughed. The harder his erection became. She had a hard time standing on her tip toes which made it hard for him to thrust like he wanted to. This just wouldn't do. The blood that had pooled at her feet caused the floor to be slick.

"You saw what you have to look forward to but first you mentioned something about screwing my brains out as we left the restaurant. Riding me hard, if I remember correctly. Well, I'm looking forward to that. Your friend managed to turn me on even more with her screaming. I'm rock hard and need some relief. But first, I have to get you primed and ready. Let's start off with some foreplay," he whispered in Becky's ear.

Becky saw the glint of the knife and tried to break free, or at least move away from it. She was tied down too tight to do either.

As he brutally raped her, he reminded the other woman that he wasn't done with her. She still had more to come. He bent down to lick a drop of blood from one of Becky's wounds. This excited him even more.

"Mmm, it's too bad you can't taste it."

Even though he moved in and out of her frantically, his erection continued to throb something fierce. It made him thrust even harder. He didn't care if it was too much for the woman. When he could no longer thrust as hard and fast as he wanted to, he used the knife in replacement of his own manhood. He started to fantasize about taking her from behind, but he couldn't chance loosening the restraints right now. He still hadn't broken her completely yet. He didn't want her to attempt escape and would wait until she passed out again.

"I'm going to treat you like the bitch dog that you are. Get on all fours." Her arms felt a momentary release as he lowered the restraints, only until he strapped her to the wall.

The Hunter picked up the whip and started to whip her fiercely as he took her from behind. He only stopped long enough to throw the condom off. He craved to feel the silkiness of her. The condom threw off his sensations. He wanted to feel every quiver her body made.

He looked over at Becky and snickered. "Don't worry; I'm not done with you. You will have another turn soon enough. There is no reason to be jealous."

While in the throes of passion, he never realized that his partner had passed out. Her body was mangled and bloody. He checked for a pulse, it was there but faint.

"Guess I'll have to switch to you won't I, Becky? It's your turn to be my dog and she'll have to be my slave. My hard on is still strong for you. This one is merely a girl and can't make me feel the way you do."

* * *

Becky couldn't believe any of this. Had she actually planned on having sex with this sick pervert? She fought back the tears. She wanted to live and make something out of her life.

She couldn't help but watch what he had done to that girl. She feared this was the serial killer everyone in the restaurant had been talking about. He looked so normal. Now, he had revealed his true persona. Evil surrounded him and threatened to swallow them whole. He had created his own hell right here in this room.

Becky knew she would be next. It was inevitable. This may be her only chance of escape. As if reading her mind, he cut the soles of her feet deeply. Next he punched her square in the face.

Chapter 76

Dan Ellis watched the time closely as he wondered where Renee was. It had been a long day and he was ready to go to sleep. He wouldn't go to sleep until she made it home. She may be a grown woman, but she was his baby after all. It wasn't like her not to call and let him know she would be late. Her phone kept going straight to voice mail. She had a bad habit of letting the battery die on the blasted thing. What good was it to have a cell phone if you didn't keep the thing charged?

He decided to call Sheriff Matthews to ask if one of his deputies could be on the lookout for her car. The sheriff lived a few doors down and they had become close friends over the years. They even talked about retiring and enjoying their golden years fishing instead of stressing over work. The houses weren't built close together, which in his mind made it a perfect neighborhood. Everyone had a nice sized lot and the back of the houses overlooked the bayou. He built a pier in the back where he could tie off his boat and launch from right there.

***

Deputy Thomas saw Renee's car broken down on the side of the road. He placed a call to the sheriff and they couldn't help but fear the worst.

This was the first time a potential victim was someone Sheriff Matthews knew personally. He dreaded breaking the news to Dan Ellis. She was a true daddy's girl and the light of his life.

Sheriff Matthews called Dan Ellis for some more information. They needed to know what time she got off of work and what time she was usually home. Perhaps she would stop by the restaurant or a bar on her way home.

Chapter 77

Elaine Anderson became annoyed when Becky didn't show up for work on Saturday and just plain aggravated when she didn't show up Sunday. These young girls nowadays believe that they could just walk out on these jobs. She thought Becky would be different. She had been proven wrong.

She placed another help wanted sign in the window. Maybe she should stop hiring young girls all together, they were just so undependable. The only problem with that was the young, pretty girls were what brought in the younger men. There seemed to be more men than women in this little town. There were also the weekenders who came out to hunt, but they still had to eat and had money to spend.

Chapter 78

Nightfall fast approached. The sunset painted a portrait across the bayou's horizon in a blaze of colors to give the day a spectacular end.

Sheriff Matthews had been dreading this phone call. "Is it Renee Ellis?"

"Yes sir, Detective Sanders is fairly certain that it is. Unfortunately, there is another body with her that we still don't have a possible ID on."

Sheriff Matthews had to break the news to Dan Ellis right away, before someone called or stopped by to see if he had heard. Dan deserved to hear it from him. When Dan greeted him at the door, he doubted Dan had slept a wink since Renee went missing.

"*Mon ami,* I'm so sorry but we found Renee. She won't be coming home."

"How bad is it? Was it the serial killer that's been on the news? I knew I should have started taking her to work. I hated her working nights."

"I am so sorry, Dan. You can't blame yourself. I'm the one to blame. I haven't been able to catch this bastard."

Chapter 79

Alex Hamilton was trying to think like the killer. He had to focus on what happened to these poor girls. He needed to get inside this killer's mind if they were ever going to catch him.

The names on the murder board were starting to get longer. Hopefully they wouldn't run out of room before he was caught.

Murder Board

Victim

Sarah Metzger
DM – October 2
DOD – October 3
Carpet fibers from possible Ford van

Marilyn Hennessey
DM – November 3
DOD – November 5
No Trace evidence found on/near body

Andrea Smith
DM – November 20
DOD – November 23
Trace amount of semen found ON body

Whitney Guillory
DM – December 5
DOD – December 8

Danielle Taylor
DM – December 15
DOD – December 16

Erica Singley
DM = December 21
DOD – December23

Sam Harrington
Last seen December 31
DOD – Jan 2

Jessica Livingston
Last seen February 13
DOD February 14

Amber Comeaux and Nicky Bryant
Last seen February 21
DOD February 23

Kathleen Landry and Diane Berkley
Last seen
February 28
DOD March 2

Sandy Ohr
DM April 15
DOD April 16

Jane Doe
DM -- UKN
DOD April 27

Renee Ellis
DM April 25
DOD April 27

Location

Undetermined
Secluded
Isolated
Possible hunting camp

Unsub

Mid 30's
Possibly drives Ford van, possibly white in color
Caucasian
6 feet, plus ???
Well-built
In shape
Financially well off or unemployed
Sexual dysfunction

Personality

Cunning
Superiority complex

Method of Killing

Torture
Rape/sexual assault: pre and post mortem
Breast mutilation
Cleaning body after death with bleach and acid

Chapter 80

Jordan walked into the sheriff's office this morning with a huge chip on her shoulder. "I don't even want to know if I have another for your eyes only note. This guy needs to go back to the hell he came from."

As Mindy handed her the note, she was already apologizing. "I'm so sorry my dear."

"I really hate this perp. I don't even want to open it."

Soon, we will meet.
Signed,
The Hunter

Alex did not look happy at all. "You are not allowed to go anywhere by yourself until this perp is caught."

Before she could even argue, Sheriff Matthews chimed in. "I agree. This guy is focusing on you way too much."

Chapter 81

The mood inside Rosy's Diner was a somber one. One of the latest victims had been a waitress here. Even though she was new to the area, everyone gathered to mourn her death. A collection basket was passed around the restaurant to send to her family to help cover funeral expenses.

Chapter 82

Jordan was not only beautiful but smart and ambitious.
Sheriff Matthews knew she wanted to be sheriff one
day. Unfortunately, she would have a lot of obstacles
to overcome. Many in this town believed the sheriff
should be a man.

She was definitely driven. She could handle the job,
maybe more than anyone else on the force or the
town for that matter. Hell, she already wanted to use
herself as bait to catch this perp. But he would not
allow that to happen. He couldn't believe Alex even let
her mention it.

With the reporters already demanding more answers
after the latest murder, he needed to bring the mayor
and D.A. up to speed before another press conference
was held. Everyone agreed to keep Jordan out of the
limelight for this one. Seeing her at the press
conference was what the perp wanted.

This killer was damn brazen about his disposal sites.
Now, with him communicating with Jordan, he was
playing some kind of game that only he knew the rules
to. He definitely had a superiority complex.

Chapter 83

A rush of desire overcame Alex as he watched Jordan sleep. He gently kissed the middle of her back, slowly waking her.

"Good morning beautiful."

"Mm, did you want some breakfast?"

"I'm looking at it."

"You don't think this is causing a problem do you?"

As he nibbled on her ear, he answered, "You think too much. Just enjoy this."

Letting out almost a purr, she informed him. "If you keep that up I won't be able to think."

"See, my plan is working."

Jordan had to keep telling herself that it was just sex. She was not falling in love with him. Just because he spent most of his nights here at her house didn't mean anything.

"You know you don't need to keep paying for a room at the local B&B. It's not like we are hiding it. You never sleep there anyway. The whole town knows you are staying here. Your rental car is usually parked right out front. Besides, we can tell everyone you decided to be my bodyguard."

"If you are positive about this I can pick up the rest of my stuff tonight."

Kissing him deeply, she told him, "I'll help."

They stopped off at a little bakery in town on the way to the office this morning. They served hot coffee and some delicious little concoctions to eat. The muffins were divine and the danishes pure heaven. They even offered cakes to buy by the slice or whole. Between Rosy's Diner and Sweet Treats, Alex could gain a lot of weight if he didn't watch it. Plus there was a little place called The Dive that served some of the best burgers he'd ever had. He didn't know why he ever worried about starving to death in this little town. It had some of the best food he'd had in a long time.

Every now and then someone would drop food off at the station to keep the officers fed. He'd never found this kind of hospitality on cases he'd worked before. He was beginning to fall in love with this quaint little town.

Chapter 84

Between the nightmares and the worrying, Sheriff Matthews couldn't sleep at night. He constantly worried about another female being abducted, tortured, and killed.

He was also concerned about Jordan. At least Hamilton was keeping a close eye on her. He wasn't thrilled about their relationship. Mindy kept reminding him she was a grown woman and it was none of his business. They needed to catch this psychopath, and fast, so life could try to get back to normal around here.

Sheriff Matthews woke up in a foul mood. He didn't know if any amount of coffee would help. The lack of sleep was catching up to him.

***

Jordan came breezing in looking all chipper. Her smile confirmed that they were more than sleeping together; he was willing to bet she was falling in love with Alex.

She quickly gathered the team together. "Let's go over this information again. Let's see if we are missing something."

After four hours, they came up with the same conclusions as before. They were dealing with one sick individual. No suspects and not enough evidence. The unsub had started to douche his victims with acid to make sure the semen was obliterated.

"Sheriff, Mr. Hennessey is calling again," announced Mindy.

He sighed as he picked up the phone, "Hello sir. I honestly wish I had some news to report to you. We are doing everything we can to find your wife's killer."

"I understand. I had hoped with the recent murders there may be some clues as to his identity. I won't keep you. I know you have work to do. Thanks again."

He looked forward to the day he could tell Mr. Hennessey and all other victims loved ones that the killer had indeed been caught. Unfortunately, right now there was nothing he could say or do that would ease the pain.

Chapter 85

Rain slowly made its way across the morning sky as Jordan woke up. It was so cozy being in bed with Alex, but she needed to get going.

She and Alex spent most of the night making love. Unfortunately, if she wanted to stay in shape she had to get out of bed and get a move on.

Alex groaned and pulled her down to him, "You know, you could do your morning calisthenics right here. Besides, it's raining outside."

"Mm, I would love to. For some reason I haven't been faithfully doing my morning run." Looking at him slyly she added, "Since there are no 24 hour gyms here, I need to try to keep fit in some way. The treadmill isn't as much fun. By the time I get home at night running is the last thing on my mind. You can come with me if you want, or are you afraid of a little rain?"

"Maybe another morning. This bed is nice and warm. Don't forget your phone and revolver, just in case this sicko really is watching your every move."

She put on her running clothes and headed out. The street lights let off a warm orange glow helping keep the darkness at bay, but daybreak wasn't far off. The rain had turned into a heavy mist that started to make its way through her clothes.

An oppressive gloom hung over the town. Porch lights lit up the neighborhood. It wasn't that long ago, before the recent horror show, that residents would be walking their dogs by now. With the recent abductions and murders no one dared to venture out anymore. She couldn't blame them though.

***

The Hunter was on his way back to his boat when he heard someone running his way. He froze but only for a moment. Who would be out in this weather besides him of course? He ducked into some brush to see who was coming. His gun was ready, just in case.

To his delight, there was *mon douce* Detective in all her glory. Even better, her lover boy was not around. And here he was without all his tools to capture his prey. It appeared he should also stalk her in the early morning hours, just in case this was a ritual he'd somehow overlooked.

***

Once again, Jordan had an eerie feeling that she was being watched. She was glad she'd listened to Alex and brought her revolver. Yet, it wouldn't protect her if he surprised her from behind. After all, Andrea had been out running when she was abducted. Maybe she should run on the treadmill, at least till he was caught. Not that she was scared, but it was better to be safe than sorry.

The wonderful smell of bacon welcomed her as soon as she opened the front door. Her stomach let out a loud rumble. She must be hungrier than she thought.

"You cooked? A girl could get used to this you know."

"I figured you would work up an appetite. Besides, I need you to keep up your strength."

"I'm starving. I've been thinking; maybe there is a way to set a trap for our guy. When I was out running I had a feeling I was being watched. If we could set up an ambush while I am on my morning run, it may just work."

"We have already had this argument. I don't like the idea of you setting a trap with this psycho and using yourself as bait," Alex argued with her.

"This may give us a really good chance to capture him though."

"I am completely against it. No matter how well you think you have it planned out, something can always go awry. This is one slick unsub. The sheriff will be against it too."

Chapter 86

Carly Granger enjoyed her job at the DA's office. Right now she worked as a receptionist, but she planned to become a legal assistant. She couldn't believe that it took her seven years to figure out what she wanted to do with her life. Now she had to convince her husband to let her take some night courses. This serial killer had him overly protective of her right now. If she didn't answer her cell phone on the second ring, she swore he would have a heart attack.

She planned to run over to the grocery store to grab a few things for supper and then check her mail before heading home. Josh had already let her know he had to work late which gave her time to catch up on some of her chores.

Just as Carly turned down the road to their house, she heard a distinct noise that could only come from a flat tire. *Great, I must have picked up a nail from somewhere.* Changing tires was one of her least favorite things, and of course there was never anyone out this way.

***

Regan Murphy had to earn a little extra cash to help with the expensive college books. She had been delivering for Flowers-N-More for two months. The job didn't pay well, but some customers would slip her a tip when she delivered flowers. The owner should invest in another delivery van since this one was on its last leg. She had to say a quick prayer each time that the minivan would start. She was at least grateful it was a minivan and not one of those huge vans. She would have preferred to use her own car, but was told no. She had to drive the company van since the company logo was on it. Supposedly it helped to promote business. *Whatever.*

The van was being funny again by not wanting to start. Her last delivery wasn't home and of course the van would break down on a road with very few houses. She should have been late for work and ran back into the house to get her phone. Now she would have to walk and hope she found someone that could help her.

***

The fog from the pain was lifting. Carly's mind began to clear. All that remained was a dull ache. The pain wasn't near as bad now. She saw the other girl chained to the wall. Who was she? She didn't look familiar. The other girl was naked, just like her. Blood had started to pool on the floor by her. What happened to her?

"What's your name?"

She didn't respond. The girl appeared to be alive, but possibly unconscious. Carly looked down and saw she was strapped to a damn chair and could not break free, no matter how hard she tried. She even tried to fold her hands to allow them to slip out, but nothing worked. Her legs were spread wide open and at any other time she would be mortified. This wasn't a good omen. She had to find a way to escape.

She could already feel her skin chafing from the tightness of the restraints. Her legs began to cramp from being in the same position for such a long period of time.

She heard footsteps and watched in the mirror as he entered. If he was allowing them to see his face, he had no plans on keeping them alive. She feared from the position he had her restrained in he wasn't going to merely torture her, eventually he would rape her.

Fury raged through her right now, not fear. "What kind of twisted game is this you son of a bitch? You can't get a woman any other way than to kidnap her? You can't get sex except to force yourself on someone? What have you already done to that poor girl? She's almost comatose!"

"Don't worry. It's your turn. You are getting ready to find out. I'm thinking I need to shut your mouth first though since you can't keep it shut. I promise you that it won't be a pleasant experience."

He forced her to "rinse" her mouth out with some acid. She refused to give up though and glared at him the whole time he stitched her mouth shut.

Pointing at Carly, he snarled out, "Let's find out if you are ready to play." He looked back towards the other woman, "Of course, she won't be as beautiful as a masterpiece as you either. You will be displayed together though. One weak and one strong. She's too close to death right now and needs to rest. She can just sit there and watch me work. Perhaps she will learn how to be strong like you."

He grabbed her face to force her to look at the other girl. "See, she is still alive. You can barely make out her heartbeat."

As he moved closer to the other girl, she started to whimper. "Tsk, tsk, tsk. It's not nice to lie."

"Please, I'm begging you to let us go. I want my daddy."

The whimpering moans intensified and turned into piercing screams as he kicked the poor girl. The screams echoed throughout the room, bouncing off the mirrors.

Carly's heart ached for this young girl. She was furious with him for tormenting her like he did.

"Stop your whining. You are pathetic."

***

Sobs racked through her body as tears flowed from the young girl. Her life was about to end, a life that was just starting. She wished for a chance to see her parents one more time. If only she could tell her little brother she was sorry for never having time for him. She regretted never letting her parents know she wasn't always a problem child. That she did listen to them. Tears continued to flow down her face and mix with the blood. Why didn't this monster just end it?

She prayed for death to come, but it didn't. The pain and suffering continued.

At first she thought the screams were coming from someone else, but they were indeed her screams. The torture intensified with her screams. Before she knew it, he had glued and sewn her mouth shut. Now all she could do was moan. She tried desperately not to make any noise, hoping he would lose interest.

* * *

He could feel the woman's body growing weaker. It became harder to revive her. He was impressed the woman made it all day. He was getting tired and needed to rest a while. This would give her a chance to build up some strength. He tortured her as much as the younger girl, but this one was strong. She was still hanging on. Not the girl though. He watched as the life left her eyes.

The Hunter wasn't sure how long he had been asleep when he lunged out of bed. He looked at the clock and realized he'd slept longer than he intended. His thoughts grew deadlier with each passing minute. The need to torture burned deep in his soul. It was time to wake his captive. He would break her will. He woke up with an erection and he had the cure for it chained to the wall in the next room.

His captive's screams had sent a euphoria over him earlier. The cloying scent of blood filled the air. The need was burning deep inside of him to punish the stubborn woman. Women were merely demons in disguise and must be banished from this world.

His control was slipping; a dark storm raged inside of him. He must gain control of his emotions. He couldn't let the darkness take over him. When he looked down at the carnage of her body, he realized he had lost complete control again. There was blood everywhere. He always prided himself on being so careful, to keep the wounds where the blood slowly escaped the body. It made clean up easier and kept his prey alive longer.

He had to be in better control of his emotions. He couldn't afford to keep losing control like this. He may eventually slip up and make a *faux pas* if he wasn't more careful. He looked at his final work. He somehow managed to turn the carnage into a piece he was proud of. This latest masterpiece was flawless.

All of his senses came to life between the hunt and the kill. It was like nothing else he had ever experienced.

Chapter 87

Jordan woke up to the sound of a phone ringing. "Sanders."

"Sorry to wake you but we have two more bodies."

"What? He just can't keep a schedule can he? What's the address and can you please call Detective Johnson for me?"

"Will do. I'll also call the sheriff."

She hung up and rolled over to wake Alex. "We have two more bodies. He's starting to like these double killings. This guy is all over the place with his kills."

"The news conference may have set him off. He is taunting us. He may also be losing control."

***

When Sheriff Matthews arrived he could barely distinguish that it was a woman's body. As he moved closer he was almost certain it was at one time, but he still wouldn't bet on it. The bodies were in such bad shape he had to take a moment and look away as bile traveled up his throat.

The smell of death hung heavy in the air, even after the bodies had been removed. His deputies looked at him with a grimness that he understood. Two more nude bodies, tortured and mutilated beyond recognition were discovered. This sick freak posed these poor women as some kind of art work. For some insane reason, he considered them as his masterpieces.

The bodies were mutilated so badly that the families would not be allowed a viewing. They should remember their loved ones before the abduction and murder. These women would not want to be remembered this way. No one should have to witness what this monster put these girls through. The pain, the terror, they surely suffered. Their families and loved ones especially didn't need to see that sight.

Everyone could all agree that whoever was committing these heinous crimes was either from Hope or connected to Hope in some way. This person knew this town and knew how to blend in here.

Murder Board

Victim

Sarah Metzger
DM – October 2
DOD – October 3
Carpet fibers from possible Ford van

Marilyn Hennessey
DM – November 3
DOD – November 5
No trace evidence found on/near body

Andrea Smith
DM – November 20
DOD – November 23
Trace amount of semen found ON body

Whitney Guillory
DM – December 5
DOD – December 8

Danielle Taylor
DM December 15
DOD – December 16

Erica Singley
DM -December 21
DOD – December23

Sam Harrington
Last seen December 31
DOD – Jan 2

Jessica Livingston
Last seen February 13
DOD February 14

Amber Comeaux and Nicky Bryant
Last seen February 21
DOD February 23

Kathleen Landry and Diane Berkley
Last seen
February 28
DOD March 2

Sandy Ohr
DM April 15
DOD April 16

Becky Griffith
DM -- UKN
DOD April 27

Renee Ellis
DM April 25
DOD April 27

Jane Doe 2 and Jane Doe 3
DM – UKN
DOD – May 14

Unsub

Mid 30's
Possibly drives Ford van, possibly white in color
Caucasian
6 feet, plus ???
Well-built
In shape
Financially well off or unemployed
Sexual dysfunction

Personality

Cunning
Superiority complex

Method of Killing

Torture
Rape/sexual assault : pre and post mortem
Breast mutilation
Cleaning body after death with bleach and acid

Chapter 88

Jordan heard Mindy call her name. "You have another note."

Until we meet, I hope you enjoy this masterpiece.
From,
The Hunter

Jordan couldn't wait until they met, with him in a jail cell. How did he send these notes without leaving behind any trace evidence? It was almost as if he prepared them in a bubble. The paper was a generic paper and the notes were printed off a printer anybody would have at home. He even started using different drop off boxes in different cities.

 Alex sensed the stress of the day was getting to her and suggested they go out to supper. Over supper, they both just enjoyed the meal, and each other.

Jordan enjoyed teasing Alex under the table. She couldn't wait to get him home and peel those clothes off of him. Her desire for him became so heavy that it was heating her blood to a boiling point. Every little touch and look caused her blood to heat up more.

The waitress stopped by to ask, "Did y'all want dessert?"

Alex answered, "Just the check please."

It quickly became a race to see who could get back to the house the fastest. They arrived home in record time and their clothes came off almost before the door even closed.

Alex traced the areola of her breast, sending shivers of desire down her spine. One hand continued to move down, gently exploring. It was more than she could take.

"Please, Alex. I need you now."

"Mm, I think I need to tease you a little more for teasing me so much in the restaurant. You were lucky I could get up from the table."

Alex thoroughly enjoyed kissing her, tasting her. Jordan writhed for release. The need became too much, the ache was deep inside. As his fingers caressed even deeper, waves of pure orgasmic pleasure coursed through her body. It wasn't enough though. She wanted him deep inside of her.

Alex rolled Jordan on top of him. They moved faster and faster with a need neither could describe until they both found their release and climaxed. Jordan was floating on cloud nine. She didn't want Alex to let her go, now or maybe ever. The realization hit her fast and hard. She had never felt like this before.

Chapter 89

This would be his riskiest capture yet. The Hunter began to grow bored once again. He needed to take a bigger risk. This was a busy neighborhood, especially in the morning.

He had been observing his recent prey for the last few days. He had known no one would pay attention to a utility worker in the area.

The daughter and her friend would catch the school bus in the morning. Afterwards the two women would have their morning coffee and chat, most likely neighborhood gossip. He remembered his mom and her friends gossiping like old biddies all the time, of course in his house it was over wine and not coffee.

He would have to act fast. He would back up the van to the garage, but the tricky part would be loading both women into the van without being noticed. An old busy body probably watched everything that went on in this neighborhood.

***

Alexis Brady never thought her life would have turned out this way. She had a wonderful and loving husband; a daughter that is her whole world. It was hard to believe that last year their whole life changed. Alexis just turned 30 and conquered breast cancer. She could take on anything now. Sure, she still had a few problems, but in the grand scheme of things she was lucky to be alive.

Without the help of her best friend, Anna Lee Adams, she would not have stayed strong for her family. They had been friends since the age of five. They even managed to get married right about the same time as well as having their daughters just a few days apart.

Tom had been great through the whole breast cancer experience, but Anna Lee had been her rock. She refused to allow her to give up.

As usual, Anna Lee and her daughter were at the kitchen door, knocking. Opening the door, she greeted her guests. "Good morning Emma Jean. Are you ready for school?"

"Yes ma'am."

Alexis looked at the time and informed her daughter, "Sally, hurry up with your breakfast. The bus will be here any minute." Looking over at her best friend, she said, "I'll brew the coffee while you get them on the bus. Then we can sit and talk."

Anna Lee nodded her head, "Come on girls, let's go. I'll be right back."

A few minutes later, Anna Lee returned. As she poured herself a cup of coffee she asked, "Alexis, did you hear about those bodies being found? I heard they don't have a clue as to who is killing these women. They suspect it is even someone from here."

"No, seriously. I just can't imagine someone from here

being a killer. Where did you hear it from?”

“We had dinner at Rosy’s Diner last night. That’s all everyone is talking about.”

“I remember glancing at an article in the paper but I didn’t pay much attention. Come on, this is Hope after all. Nothing ever happens here. Besides, it’s not like we go partying at night. Hell, half the time I never leave the house.”

“Are you expecting someone? A van just backed in.”

“I don’t think so. Tom didn’t say anything this morning about having work done.”

***

The Hunter had his stun guns ready. He rang the doorbell and waited.

“Good morning, can I help you?”

The first woman went down fast. She never had time to scream.

“Alexis, you okay honey?” The second woman screamed as soon as she saw her friend on the floor and the man closing the door.

“Quickly, I believe your friend passed out.”

She wasn’t falling for it and took off. Acting fast, he grabbed her by the hair and aimed the stun gun. He caught her on her way down.

Moving quickly, he had both handcuffed and zip tied their legs. He was glad he had backed the van up to the garage. After opening the garage door, he carefully looked around to make sure that no one was watching. He opened the van doors and dropped both women in unceremoniously. He secured each pair of handcuffs to a special latch he had welded to the van. They should stay out until he made it to the cabin, but he always liked to be prepared.

***

Emma Jean didn't see her mother outside. She always waited outside for the bus. She or Sally's mother always greeted them with smiling faces. They always asked the girls if they had a good day at school, or some other corny question. Neither one was outside, though.

"Sally, where are our moms?"

"Maybe they are inside and didn't notice the time. Besides, I heard mom telling dad that she was tired this morning."

The bus driver honked his horn to let the moms know he was here as he let the girls out. Sally tried the front door, but it was locked. They went around to the back door, but discovered that it was locked also.

"Come on; let's go see if Mrs. Mavis is home. Maybe she'll let me call Dad."

Emma Jean said, "We can go to my house."

"Nah, that's on the other street. Besides, Mrs. Mavis will have cookies, she always has cookies. We'll see if she is home, first. We can call your house to see if they are over there. Besides, maybe one of our moms left a message with her."

When Mrs. Mavis opened the door, Sally asked, "Mrs. Mavis, have you seen either of our moms? No one is answering the door and they are all locked."

"No sweethearts I haven't."

"Do you mind if we use your phone to call our moms' cell phone or at least Dad? Maybe he knows something."

"Come on in, I have some cookies. You are more than welcome to use the phone."

They called both of their mother's cell phones with no luck. There was no answer at Emma Jean's house either.

Sally called her dad, "Daddy, is mom okay? She isn't home."

"She should be. She planned on being lazy today. Sally, let me talk to Mrs. Mavis please."

"Martha, it's Tom. Have you seen Alexis today?"

"I haven't seen her all day. The only thing I noticed over there today was the telephone worker."

"What telephone worker? We weren't having any problems," he asked anxiously.

"Oh my, he got there sometime after the bus came. I don't think he was over there even an hour. By the time I looked back out, he was gone."

"Can the girls stay over there please? I am leaving the office right now to come home."

"Well of course they can."

***

Tom called William Adams at work, "Do you know where Anna Lee or Alexis is at?"

"They should be at your house waiting on the kids."

"Well they aren't and Alexis isn't answering her phone. I'm heading over to the house now."

"I'll call Anna Lee's cell phone and the house. I'll also try her mother's. I'll let you know if I get in touch with her."

Tom let his secretary know he was heading home. "Keep trying my wife please. Let me know if you get in touch with her and have her call me too. I'm heading home now."

"Yes sir."

It took at least 45 minutes for him to get home, depending on traffic. He contemplated whether or not to ask Sheriff John Matthews to run to the house and check things out. Finally, he pulled out his phone.

"John, its Tom Brady. I have a favor to ask of you. Alexis and Anna Lee didn't get the girls off the bus this afternoon. Depending on traffic, I'm still about 45 minutes away. Martha Mavis saw a telephone worker over there this morning, but she hasn't seen the women. I didn't schedule anyone to come out to the house today, and Alexis wasn't feeling well, so she had talked about going back to bed. She never mentioned a worker coming out today. Would you mind checking things out for me please? Maybe Alexis just fell asleep and forgot to set her alarm for when the girls came home. Martha has a spare key for emergencies."

"Sure, no problem."

***

"Sanders, let's take a ride. Tom Brady can't reach his wife or her friend."

"Oh lord, but its broad daylight and that's a pretty close knit neighborhood. That doesn't sound like our unsub."

"He did strike at a mall in broad daylight. We know he is escalating. Besides, it could be nothing. I told Tom I'd check it out for him since it'll be a while before he can make it home, anyway."

"*'T'es paré*? Are you ready?"

"*Allons*. Besides, I could use some fresh air."

It took all of four minutes to get there.

"I'm going to go check around the outside of the house. You go see if Mrs. Mavis has the key. For some reason the old bat hates me."

Jordan just laughed, "No problem."

She went next door and knocked on Mrs. Mavis's door.

"Tom had called to tell me you would be stopping by. Here's the key. I sure hope everything is all right."

"I'm sure it is. I'll return it shortly."

Jordan rushed back. "Here's the key sir."

"Let's go in armed just in case. You stay low, I'll go high."

"Sounds good to me."

"Mrs. Brady. It's John, Sheriff Matthews. Tom is worried since you aren't answering your phone. He asked that I come over. Anna Lee, are you here too?" Sheriff Matthews asked into the house.

Nothing but dead silence greeted him.

"It smells like burnt coffee, sir," Jordan pointed out.

"It also appears that a skirmish took place over here." Sheriff Matthews noticed heading into the kitchen. "Things are knocked over. I have a bad feeling about this. Jordan, call in the crime scene techs just to be safe."

"Yes sir."

He continued to look around, he heard Jordan on the phone.

"Mindy, it's Jordan. Can you send the crime scene techs to the Brady residence? I'll call Agent Hamilton so that he can dispatch the FBI."

"Agent Hamilton, its Detective Sanders. It appears that we may have another potential abduction. The address is 121 Cypress Street. It's not too far from the command center. You may want to send the whole team just in case."

Sheriff waited until she was off the phone and gave Jordan further instructions. "We need to get in touch with William Adams to check out his house too. I think this is our crime scene though. I'm assuming that they were abducted during morning coffee. I'll call Tom to get William's number. Plus, I'm sure he will want some answers." Sheriff Matthews dreaded calling Tom, but he needed to get in touch with William as soon as possible.

"Tom, it's John. We are at your house. Can you give me William's number? We want to go check out his house too."

"I take it they weren't over at the house then," sheriff could hear the fear in Tom's voice as he answered.

He felt no need to inform Tom that a struggle took place and that the coffee pot had been left on. "No, I'm sorry but Alexis and Anna Lee weren't over here. We aren't giving up. Detective Sanders and I want to check the other house to make sure they aren't over there."

"I'll text you his contact info now. They don't usually go over there though. Alexis doesn't like to leave the house much. She's more comfortable at home lately."

"I understand that Tom, but it's better to be safe." With that, he hung up the phone and waited for the text to come through.

When he got the phone number, he quickly called William Adams. "William, it's Sheriff Matthews. I'm guessing Tom has told you what's going on?"

"Yes sir. They aren't at his house I take it."

"No, can we have your permission to check out your house?" he asked.

"Sure, there is a spare key taped under the porch light. I'm leaving work now."

Sheriff Matthews wanted to warn him about the chances he was taking leaving a spare key lying around outside, but the poor man probably had enough guilt eating at him right now. Why make him feel any worse than he already did?

"We will see you soon. Let us check things out before you go home."

"Yeah, sure, no problem."

There were no signs of either woman at Anna Lee and William's house. No signs that Anna Lee had returned home after bringing Emma Jean over to the Brady household.

Sheriff Matthews had a bad feeling about this. The women seemed to have vanished. If it was their guy, he was definitely getting more brazen.

The crime scene techs and FBI were arriving when Sheriff Matthews and Sanders returned from the Adams' house. They both knew it was best to step back and let these guys work. To make themselves at least feel useful, they cordoned off the house just to be safe. Maybe this time they would gather some evidence to catch this guy.

Tom arrived just as everyone was getting started. He was completely pale as he got out of his truck. "What's going on now? Have you heard any more news?"

Sheriff went over to talk to him. "Just as a precaution

we are working this as a crime scene. Let the team do their job. Let's see if they can find anything to help us locate Alexis and Anna Lee."

"You don't think it's that psycho do you?"

"Let's not jump to conclusions right now. That won't help anyone at all. I'm praying that he isn't involved. This isn't his usual MO."

As the residents slowly came out of their homes, the sheriff watched as Jordan grabbed her pen and pad. This may be the best time to find out if anyone noticed anything at all. If these women were kidnapped this morning, the kidnapper had a good eight hour head start.

"Well, get anything?" Sheriff asked when she made her way back to him.

"Several neighbors reported seeing a white van, maybe from the telephone company. They figured they were having phone problems and didn't pay much attention."

"Damn, that may be how he is going unnoticed. He really does blend in."

***

Alexis began to pray. After all, prayer helped her beat breast cancer. She couldn't believe that she was meant to survive breast cancer only to be killed by some raving maniac. She could make out shallow breathing noises coming from Anna Lee so she was still alive, at least for now.

Alexis knew in her heart of hearts that this was the same killer that Anna Lee had talked about this morning. She felt the van stop. She had a sinking suspicion they had arrived at the place where he planned to kill them.

As the man opened the van doors, light poured in. Alexis knew they didn't travel long. It still felt like the morning sun outside and there was still a chill in the air. The afternoon sun hadn't begun to heat up the remainder of the day.

When he grabbed at Alexis she desperately began to kick. His touch made her recoil in fear. His eyes were so dark and so ominous. Hatred burned right through her. She didn't even recognize the man. What did she ever do to him?

"Why are you doing this? I don't even know you!"

He just snickered.

"Please, God, I'm not ready to die. Help me." She was in the presence of the devil himself.
.

*** *

As Anna Lee came to, she swore she heard a woman crying. "Alexis, is that you honey?" When she saw her naked reflection in the mirror she screamed out, "Oh God, where are we?"

She shivered from the cold or possibly from fear, perhaps both, she wasn't sure. She blinked rapidly, still trying to focus her eyes. She needed to get a better view of her surroundings. After things became clearer, she realized she was better off not being able to see clearly.

Alexis stopped crying. "Oh, Anna Lee, it's awful. We've been kidnapped. He has us captive in some kind of room. I can't move." Forcing back her sobs she asked, "Anna Lee, you don't think it's that killer that has us do you?"

"God, let's pray not."

Her arms and legs refused to move. She was restrained.

When she heard footsteps approaching, her stomach dropped as fear took over. This had to be a really bad dream. She needed to wake up. She tried to remember what happened. How did she end up here? How long was she out?

Once he entered the room, she knew they were doomed. No amount of prayer would save them. She couldn't stop the tears from streaming down her face.

"Now that you're awake, I need to fix your eyes. Then, of course, we can begin."

Pain shot through her. She tried to break free with everything she had left in her body.

Fear tore through Anna Lee's body. She couldn't stop shaking. His eyes gleamed with malice as he probed her with the knife. The cuts were just deep enough to bleed, but not deep enough to kill her. The pain was excruciating. She continued to pray. "Lord, please give me the strength to endure this. If I am to die, please let it be quick."

This man was completely psychotic. A truly demented, twisted soul who was evil reincarnated.

In horror, she watched as he touched her body. She felt the cold sting of the knife blade enter her body. Blood oozed out of each cut and slowly puddled on the floor. He grew hard with excitement.

A pure visceral fear coursed through her body, from her head to her toes. She tried to block out the screaming, the awful screaming, coming from Alexis. It was impossible though. She couldn't stop the tears as reality set in. She was next.

She tried to keep the terror building inside of her from showing through in her eyes and hide the way fear caused her body to tremble. She refused to give him that satisfaction.

This wasn't going to end well for her or her friend. A deep sense of dread washed over her. This time she would die, and it would be by someone else's hand. She always thought it would be the cancer that killed her. The cancer would have been a less painful death.

Chapter 90

Alexis Brady's neighborhood was being canvassed to ask if anyone else noticed anything out of the ordinary, maybe something not quite right. The officers canvassing all reported several people seeing the white utility van, and most believed it belonged to the telephone company. Sheriff Matthews had Jordan follow-up with the telephone company. Hopefully they had a record on who was dispatched.

Unfortunately, no one thought to get a license plate number. Half of the witnesses couldn't even be certain it was even a telephone company van. Some thought it may have been a cable company van. The killer had found a perfect disguise to keep him invisible during the day.

"Sheriff Matthews, you're not going to like this one bit. I called both the telephone and cable company, neither had any workers scheduled for work in that neighborhood. Actually, they didn't have work scheduled here this whole week. I've got a call into the electric company, but I don't think they use vans," Jordan stated.

"Damn it, I was afraid of that. Good work, though."

"I would have preferred having good news to tell you though. The telephone company did say that they sold several of their older vans a while back. They are compiling a list of people who bought them."

"I know everyone wants to keep working 24 hours

straight right now until we find Alexis and Anna Lee, but it isn't helping the case if we are all tired. I say let's take six hour shifts. It's not much, but we can at least go home to shower and catch a power nap if you are lucky.

"Hamilton and Jordan I'll leave you together. Johnson and I will take the second shift. We know this killer is around here. This damn town isn't big enough for him to hide in forever. I have the deputies driving down every road searching for a white utility van in a driveway. Maybe, just maybe, we will get lucky."

Alex looked over at Jordan, "Well, you want to take him up on the offer? Go home and take a power nap."

"I guess I should. I can barely keep my eyes open. Sheriff, why don't we make this first shift a four hour one, because I know you are tired too."

Jordan looked at Johnson when she made the statement. His eyes were already drooping and bloodshot. "No, we will be fine. You'll go home and try to get some sleep. Maybe with our minds refreshed we can come up with a plan. Besides, my kids are sleeping right now. I'd like to see them for a bit. It will be a while before they are awake."

Sheriff Matthews addressed Jordan, "Whatever plan we come up with will not involve you using yourself as bait. Another plan of attack needs to be discussed."
"Yes sir. But I still think it could work. For some reason he is fascinated with me."

Alex stated the obvious, "It's because you are a woman in control, power. He finds you an enigma."

"We have to consider the fact that it is only a matter of time before he's tired of playing games with you and moves in for the kill." Alex paused before continuing, "We have to be missing something, something right in front of our faces. I had my team run criminal records to see if there is someone living here that has prior sexual assaults that could have lead up to this. That was a bust, though."

Sheriff was taken aback by that statement, "Son, I could have told you that."

"I wasn't trying to step on any toes here. I knew you would know about local arrests, but I wanted to check on newcomers and arrests made out of your jurisdiction. We know this killer had to start somewhere.

"He has to slip up soon. The killer is escalating in the torture of these victims. His sexual assault is getting worse. The bodies are showing overkill in the mutilation. Killing just one at a time no longer satisfies his craving now, he has moved on to two women. I'm worried that with his escalation the killing of two women at once will no longer satisfy him."

"Well, as much as I would like to continue this discussion," Jordan stated with exaggerated sarcasm, "I'm going to take up the sheriff's offer and go home. I'm in serious need of a hot shower and migraine medicine."

Johnson smirked, "I thought I smelled something."

"You are just so funny. Trust me; it's not too pleasant to stand near you either."

"Just remember to set your alarm clock. We don't want you to oversleep." Johnson said with a wicked wink and a gleam in his eyes.

***

At least the joking around helped to ease some of the stress. As soon as they were in the car it was like two horny teenagers.

"Alex, you better get me home. And absolutely no talking about the case."

"Don't worry I have other things on my mind besides the case or sleep right now."

Jordan couldn't get the front door unlocked fast enough. They kissed feverishly as soon as they entered the house. Neither knew if they would be able to make it to the bedroom. Alex picked Jordan up as if she weighed nothing at all. They never broke the kiss as he carried her over to the couch, the bed could wait.

Somehow they were both undressed when they reached the living room. Legs and arms were suddenly entangled. As he kissed the sensitive area of Jordan's neck, it sent shivers down her already heated flesh.

Jordan loved the way the sinewy muscles of his body felt. She gently stroked him, and teased him the same way he teased her, with slow, languid kisses.

She melted into him. He made his way down her body with slow, gentle kisses. Time stood still when she was in his arms. Jordan could think of nothing else but him and the way he made her body sing. His tongue slipped in between her legs, caressing and stroking the very core of her being. She let out a deep moan.

"I need you. I can't wait any longer."

In one swift move he was inside her, filling her completely. Nothing else mattered except this moment.

Chapter 91

The bayou played its own special song again tonight. Crickets serenaded one another, the frogs croaked, and an alligator slipped into the water for a late night snack. With the water warming up, the alligators were moving around more. They were no longer as sluggish as they had been over the last few weeks.

Twin Oaks Plantation Home had a crawfish boil planned for that afternoon along the bayou. They invited several news reporters in hopes of possibly getting some free advertisement. The gazebo that had been built along the bayou was the perfect setting for The Hunter's latest masterpiece. The smell of the blood would surely bring the gators in for a close look. Timing was crucial for this to work. It would do no good for a gator to drag the bodies off before *mon douce* Detective got a look.

***

The catering company, Boudreaux's Seafood, arrived early that morning to set up. Jacques Boudreaux knew how to boil seafood down here and his company was always in demand. Unlike his fellow competitors he didn't just add the spices at the last minute or sprinkle boil on top. *Mais non*, that wasn't the way you boil seafood. You season the water first. It took a lot of seasonings to get the crawfish perfect. *Ça c'est bon*, that's what makes it good. He was also pleased the boil was right along the bayou. It made clean up easier. Even the fish get to enjoy his good food.

Jacques even offered Twin Oaks a break in the price in hopes of getting a little free advertising. A 'you scratch my back and I'll scratch yours' kind of deal.

The crawfish were pretty this year. They had all been nice sized and even though the season was winding down, they were still big. Everyone should have a good time and leave with their bellies full. It was time to get this boil started. As they say, *laissez les bon temps rouler*, let the good times roll.

Jacques was surprised to see someone already down at the gazebo. Someone else may be ready to party early also. At least he would have someone to share a cold one with. You couldn't boil crawfish without drinking a beer or two. As Jacques got closer, he realized it wasn't someone that was invited. *Douce mère de Mary de Dieu*. He made a sign of the cross while reaching for his phone. *Pauve ti bêtes*, who would want to do something like this.

***

Sheriff Matthews had just fallen asleep. He had been home only a short time when the blasted thing rang. It took several rings before he even realized it was the phone.

He answered the phone groggily, "Let me guess, Alexis and Anna Lee have been found? Please at least tell me it is good news."

The dispatcher dreaded being the one to inform him. "I'm sorry sir."

"I'm on my way."

When Sheriff Matthews arrived on scene things were already in a controlled chaos. The crime scene techs and FBI were there too. Somehow the news crew even managed to make it there before him. They must be camping out at the mobile command unit now waiting for them to leave.

"There's nothing like having microphones shoved in your face first thing in the morning. I just love being bombarded with questions from nosy reporters before I've even had my coffee. Everyone wants answers, but there aren't any. Please tell me that we have something to give them."

Alex walked up to him, "We may catch a break really soon. From the look of one of the bodies, he may be starting to lose control."

"We may catch a break soon, but these victims sure aren't," he stated grimly.

As the sun started to rise, he hoped the evil that had been lingering over the crime scene would dissipate in the sunlight. Perhaps it would take the darkness of the night with it.

The news crews started to leave and only a few curious town folk remained. Seventeen murders, now nineteen, and no suspects.

"I want this guy caught. I'm asking the mayor to push

the neighboring towns to increase patrols on their ends also. Let's make it harder for this guy to find victims. I don't want to keep making notifications to families and loved ones."

Sheriff Matthews looked at Jordan with weariness in his eyes. Notifying the families was actually worse than finding the body.

***

It had become very personal with Sheriff Matthews. It was hard not to. This creep killed in their backyard, right under their noses. This case was turning into a nightmare, a never ending nightmare. The body count continued to increase at an exponential rate. No one on the force could sleep at night. Everyone was on edge and had their own way of dealing with the stress.

Sheriff Matthews felt as if they were running in circles. This killer was cunning. So far, no evidence had turned up. They didn't even have an idea as to where he held these women captive. They were fairly certain he used one of the hunting camps but they couldn't prove it. It's not like a judge would issue a search warrant for all hunting camps and private homes that were isolated.

He could tell from the wounds on the victims that they were meant for a long, slow death. These women were tortured slowly. They bled out while being raped savagely. The killer applied different torture techniques to each victim. He rarely used the same group of techniques twice. The only consistencies were the eyes and mouths. They were all pried open and he glued and sewed shut the mouths on the later bodies. But then some women had acid poured down their throats and others had their teeth pulled out.

Agent Hamilton suspected that when the screaming became too much he decided to seal the mouth shut. However, at least one of the women was stated to be very opinionated. Maybe if they didn't surrender and fought, they were permanently shut up. Both were plausible explanations.

He definitely knew how to inflict pain. Agent Hamilton was positive that he didn't just start out by torturing women. He had been practicing for a while. For some reason he chose now to let his work known.

They truly believed that there were more bodies out there. They just had not been discovered or connected to this killer. They may never surface or be linked to this killer.

This was not the Anna Lee and Alexis that the sheriff knew and cared about. The women he remembered were gorgeous and vibrant. He despised that this would be how he remembered them. Now they were just a tangled mass of flesh and bones. It was hard to tell where one body ended and another started. The coroner had his work cut out for him today. Rage built up deep inside of Sheriff Matthews. It was ready to boil over at any given moment. He didn't understand how the perp continued to elude capture.

Sheriff Matthews looked over at Jordan and stated, "We have to bump up patrols and increase shifts.

Screw worrying about overtime. I want this bastard caught."

Alexis had overcome so much in her life only to be killed by a maniac. It just wasn't fair, life wasn't fair.

Jordan looked over at Sheriff Matthews. Tom and Alexis Brady were good friends with him and Mindy. This kill hit too close to home for him. She could see the sorrow in his eyes.

"Sir, we know it's the same guy. I mean the way the bodies were put on display confirms it. I know the FBI says the abduction wasn't his signature, but it is."

"I agree, the pathology is the same."

Agent Hamilton stepped in, "This is the same killer. He is showing you how proud he is with his work. It's true showmanship to him. Just like we display awards, he is displaying the bodies. He is evolving, stepping up his game, which is why the abduction was different."

Sheriff Matthews dreaded making this visit, but it was his responsibility. He had to get it over with before the news spread like wildfire and Tom heard it from someone else, or worse and saw it on the news. Names had not been released, but the press would soon report that more bodies had been found.

This unsub was beyond brazen. He showed no fear in anything he did. Sheriff Matthews hoped the crime scene techs and photographers would hurry up. He wanted to get these women moved before reporters moved in like a bunch of buzzards. They would catch this guy. This psychopath could not win, he wouldn't let him win.

These deaths were so horrific. You wouldn't even wish this on your worst enemy.

***

The Brady's house was in one of the newer subdivisions in town. It was only a mile or two from their church, where they all met.

The Brady's owned one of the more expensive homes in the city, but they never acted as if they were better than anyone else. They moved here right after Hurricane Katrina hit Louisiana. Their house was destroyed in the hurricane and Alexis didn't want to rebuild. She wanted to live in a smaller town. Ever since they moved here, Tom commuted back and forth.

Tom greeted him at the door. His eyes were red from crying. Sheriff Matthews knew it was only going to get worse. As soon as Tom saw him, he immediately broke down. His heart went out to the poor man and his daughter.

"Tom, let's move inside. I'm so sorry, I wish I had better news. I don't know what to say. Where is Sally? Is she home?"

"Alexis's mom came and got her last night so I could be ready to go in a moment's notice, you know just in case. I honestly didn't want her in the same house where her mother was abducted."

"I have a few more questions to ask you. I know Detective Sanders and others probably asked you these questions already, but maybe you'll remember something else. You're sure Alexis didn't mention anything suspicious a few days before she disappeared? Nothing at all? She didn't call the telephone or cable company?"

"No, she never mentioned anything. Sally did mention that a telephone guy had been in the neighborhood all this past week. Honestly, he could have been and I would have thought it was routine. Those vans seem to be everywhere.

"How bad was it? I always worried the cancer would take her from me, but I never in my worst nightmares considered something like this would happen."

"I know. I am so sorry, Tom. If there is anything Mindy or I can do to help you, don't hesitate to ask. Mindy will probably be bringing you over some food again today. Detective Sanders and Agent Hamilton are letting William know. I felt I had to let you know personally though."

"John, catch this bastard and let me have five minutes alone with him."

＊＊＊

Sheriff Matthews was deep in thought. He was sitting

at the conference table just staring at the murder board. Murder Board, he never thought he would have one of these in his station. Jordan was really starting to impress him. He was glad he put her in charge as lead detective. She was even outshining some of the state trooper and FBI personnel.

He'd have to watch out or they would try to steal her away. His other deputies were handling the stress of this case okay. This was something they weren't used to. Now these murders were hitting even closer to home.

After all, most of the deputies here spent their time writing tickets. You may get a call on a domestic dispute matter or bar brawl, but those were even infrequent. Especially compared to the surrounding cities and towns. Hope was usually a very peaceful place to live.

Murder Board

Victim

Sarah Metzger
DM – October 2
DOD – October 3
Carpet fibers from possible Ford van

Marilyn Hennessey
DM – November 3
DOD – November 5
No trace evidence found on/near body

Andrea Smith
DM – November 20
DOD – November 23
Trace amount of semen found ON body

Whitney Guillory
DM – December 5
DOD – December 8

Danielle Taylor
DM December 15
DOD – December 16

Erica Singley
DM -December 21
DOD – December23

Sam Harrington
Last seen December 31
DOD – Jan 2

Jessica Livingston
Last seen February 13
DOD February 14

Amber Comeaux and Nicky Bryant
Last seen February 21
DOD February 23

Kathleen Landry and Diane Berkley
Last seen
February 28
DOD March 2

Sandy Ohr
DM April 15
DOD April 16

Becky Griffith
Renee Ellis
DM April 25
DOD April 27

Carly Granger and Reagan Murphy
DM May 11
DOD May 14

Alexis Brady
Anna Lee Adams
Date Missing May 18
DOD May 20

Location

Undetermined

Secluded
Isolated
Possible hunting camp ????

Unsub

Mid 30's
Possibly drives Ford van, possibly white in color
Caucasian
6 feet, plus ???
Well-built
In shape
Financially well off or unemployed
Sexual dysfunction

Personality

Cunning
Superiority complex

Method of Killing

Torture
Rape/sexual assault: pre and post mortem
Breast mutilation
Cleaning body after death with bleach and acid

Chapter 92

The mood in the Sheriff's Office was sullen this morning. Mindy looked up from her desk, "I don't want to know what this says."

"Me neither. How is Sheriff Matthews holding up?"

"He's feeling guilty. We were such close friends with Tom and Alexis Brady."

The beauty of this masterpiece does not do your beauty justice.
From,
The Hunter

Agent Hamilton pulled Jordan aside later in the day. "I have a conference call with my team later this afternoon but I don't want you to go home without me. We can pick up a pizza on the way home?"

"That sounds good. I will go for a quick run and try to unwind while I'm waiting for you. I don't want to think about death for a while."

"Please be careful. We know he is watching your every move."

Jordan looked at her watch and couldn't believe the time. The storm clouds decided to linger even though it had stopped raining.

Looking out the window, she noticed a few people were starting to venture outside more.

She headed to the car for her extra set of shoes and clothes. She desperately craved fresh air and no talk of death.

After a few quick stretches, she took off at a slow pace. A young mom with a toddler in a stroller passed by. Jordan had found herself recently thinking of babies, families, husbands, and happily married ever after. Until she met Alex, marriage never entered her mind. All she ever thought about was her career.   Now, she was rethinking this love theory. She had never believed in love before Alex. Hell, it may not even be love she felt for Alex but instead romantic infatuation.

She never considered herself a clingy girlfriend whose life would come to an end if a guy didn't propose. Hell, she may not even make good wife material. All she knew for certain was that she couldn't wait to be alone with Alex.   She didn't see wedding bells anywhere in the near future, but she was not ready to see him leave either.

Jordan kept her speed at a leisurely pace. She was just starting to unwind when Alex called to say he was done.

Chapter 93

A late afternoon thunderstorm struck with a
vengeance. Lightning streaked across the sky as the
thunder crashed overhead. The heavy rain was mixed
with hail the size of golf balls. As Alex and Jordan
made a mad dash from the car to the house they
became drenched.

"It's really coming down all of a sudden."

"Welcome to Louisiana, where you never know what
the weather will be like from one minute to the next."

Jordan let out a deep breath. It was time for them to
regroup. They were missing something, they had to
be.

Alex came up behind her and began to massage her
shoulders. "Mm, that feels good."

He knew that you couldn't judge a book by its cover.
Jordan was a case in point. She reminded him of a pit
bull when she had her mind set. She was determined
to catch the killer. If this man did attempt to abduct
her, look out. It would be a ferocious fight, with the
killer ending up as the loser. You could see the rage in
her eyes when she received a note, taunting her.

"None of these women deserved to be tortured and
mutilated the way they were. I don't care what this
creep thinks," Jordan said.

He took her in his arms, wishing he could take all the

worry away from her face. This case was getting to everyone.

The kiss was completely sexual, carnal. He slipped his tongue in Jordan's mouth, slowly caressing and exploring. His hands ran over her body at the same time.

Chapter 94

The Hunter couldn't believe his eyes. His sweet Detective was at the grocery store. He also didn't notice the boyfriend's rental car in the parking lot. It was still too risky to try and abduct her from here, but he couldn't resist following her around the store. This gave him an opportunity to walk right by her and go unnoticed. He would even take a chance by following her home in case an opportune moment presented itself to abduct her. His pulse raced at the thought.

He found her right away. She was laughing at something a shopper must have told her. He placed a few things in his buggy to look like he was shopping.

He noticed a bottle of wine along with cheese and crackers in the buggy. She and the FBI profiler would probably enjoy a glass of wine before bed. He envisioned them talking about him and how he kept outsmarting them. As he pushed his buggy closer to her he breathed in her perfume. She smelled so damn good. Did she always wear perfume to work or was it to impress her boyfriend?

Damn, speaking of the bastard. The Hunter noticed him waltzing up to her. He overheard him say, "I found what I was looking for."

He watched as they headed to the checkout. There was no chance of abducting her tonight. They must have ridden here together, of all the rotten luck.

He would send his sweet Detective another little

present in the morning to let her know he had watched her tonight. He found a coffee shop with internet in a town a few miles over. After a quick search he located a company nearby that would deliver personalized gift baskets to Hope for a small delivery charge. Perfect, he listed the wine, cheese, crackers, and chocolate he saw in her basket.

The card read, "I saw you, but did you see me?"

He loved to taunt his sweet Detective so.

****

Not long after lunch Mindy noticed a delivery man come into the Sheriff's office. A twinge of apprehension came over her.

"I have a delivery for a Detective Jordan Sanders."

"Son, stay right there until I can get someone to take a closer look at that basket. The Sheriff will also want to speak with you. You may as well take a seat over there."

He paled and she saw a bead of sweat form on his forehead. "It's just a gift basket that I was told to deliver."

"Then you have nothing to worry about do you? We have to make sure that this is a normal delivery."

"I just deliver where my boss tells me to."

"Let's just see if anyone needs to ask you any questions."

"John, you and Jordan need to come out here. She has a delivery."

Sheriff Matthews and Jordan just looked at each other. This was a new twist. There wasn't another body found, why would he contact her now?

"Maybe it's nothing. It may not even be from him."

"*Allons.* Let's go check it out."

Luckily the card was on the outside. Using a pencil Jordan carefully opened the card. As she read it she began to shake, not with fear but with rage. As she looked at the items in the basket, she realized he must have been in the store with her last night.

"Sheriff, these are some of the exact items I bought at the store last night."

Sheriff Matthews told the delivery boy, "Son, I think it's time you called your boss. See if she knows anything about this order."

After a few moments he came back and said, "It was an internet order placed late last night. No name on the order."

Sheriff Matthews instructed Mindy. "Get the crime scene techs over to the store. Perhaps they can at least pull something off the computer."

They all knew the answer though.

Chapter 95

Alice Myers was happily married, thirty-two, and for some reason she couldn't figure out what to do with her life. She had just been promoted as manager at the local SaveMart. Unfortunately, she had the night shift. She didn't want to work there for the rest of her life. Maybe she should go back to school. She always thought it would be neat to sell houses. She was seriously considering getting her real estate license. That way she would be home at night with her husband.

Alice despised nights like this. She had a sense of foreboding all day and couldn't shake the feeling. The fog moved in fast. By the time she got off work it would be almost impossible to see what was in front of her. Ever since Black Friday, the Christmas shopping had been crazy. Parents all came in wanting a certain toy or game. The layaway lines were steadily picking up.

Maybe this was a sign that the economy was picking up. Heaven knew it was needed. She called her husband to let him know she was on her way home. It would be nice to hear his voice. All she could think about was curling up with him and falling sound asleep. When he put his arms around her it made all of her problems go away. They had talked about starting a family and maybe it was time. She wasn't getting any younger.

Alice never considered herself to be a weak woman, a coward, but there was something eerie about tonight.

The fog was so thick and seemed to be endless. Even the moon had gone into hiding.

She didn't mind driving home at night. There were usually no cars on the road at this hour. She had time to unwind on the way home from work.

The fog was getting extremely dense. It would provide the perfect cover for him. It had been a while since he was in this area. He knew the entrance was nearby.

Her husband must have been asleep so she left him a message. "Hey it's me. I'm on my way home but the fog is getting really bad. I may be a few minutes late."

The next thing Alice knew, she had rear-ended something. The airbags went off and all she saw was black afterwards. She never even saw a vehicle in front of her.

She needed to call 911 but couldn't find her phone. She should check on the other driver. Great, she couldn't afford a wreck right now. Why did she drop full coverage? This accident was entirely her fault.

As she reached for the door handle the door was jerked open. She screamed in surprise.
Alice didn't notice that right before the accident her phone was still on. It had continued to record a message on her husband's phone.

***

Alice's husband, Jack, woke up suddenly. Alice should

have been home by now. He looked at his phone and realized there was a message. He never even heard the phone ring. Maybe the store had broken its number one rule and gave her more hours. How on earth did they expect people to make a living on minimum wage and 19 hours a work week?

As he listened to the message fear overtook his senses. He heard a crash and Alice scream a little while later. Next he heard what sounded like a struggle and doors slamming.

"What the hell was going on?" He immediately called 911.

An inexplicable sense of dread came over Jack as he headed out. He should stay at home and wait instead of looking for his wife. He had to do something. He was never good at waiting.

***

The state trooper heard the call on the scanner and warning bells went off. They didn't need another missing woman. He was concerned that it could be just like in Hope. The State Trooper read the notice earlier warning everyone to be on the lookout. This guy was known to have kidnapped women from nearby cities. The second victim was not only from another city but another state. However these women just disappeared into thin air, no clues. Could they be getting lucky and he had made a mistake.

Chapter 96

As Alice opened her eyes, the veil of darkness slowly lifted. Her heart beat faster. An image flashed through her mind. She had a hard time piecing everything together. What happened? Where was she?

She heard someone calling her name, but it sounded so distant. Fear coursed through her body. She had a feeling that something horrible was about to happen.

It seemed like he thrived on fear and could smell the fear emitting from her body. Alice desperately tried to get herself under control. She refused to give him the pleasure of knowing how scared she really was.

"Go to hell."

With a wicked smile he said, "You are in hell, the hell I created just for you."

She pulled hard against the restraints in an attempt to break free. She desperately wanted to escape from this place, from him. The restraints were so tight that they cut into her skin as she pulled.

He hovered over her, carefully gluing each eye open. Next, he glued her luscious lips together and then meticulously stitched them closed. Blood seeped out of each stitch. He licked the droplets away, as if savoring the coppery taste of the blood. Her breath was raspy coming from her nose. She tried to turn her head away from him, but it was no use. She glared at him with contempt and hatred in her eyes.

"You belong to me, you are my prisoner. I will do what I want to you. You have no control over me. Get used to it."

She continued to glare at him. "We are completely secluded here. No one will come to your rescue."

There was blood everywhere. It kept getting into her eyes, and she couldn't blink it away. The pain became all consuming. If she could only slip into unconsciousness. It would stop the pain. The pain had become almost mind numbing.

Chapter 97

As the rest of the town slept, Jack went in search of his wife. He saw the flashing lights of the trooper's car before he noticed his wife's vehicle. The damage to the car didn't look too bad. Maybe it was a hit-and-run.

Still he never heard back from his wife.   Jack didn't see an ambulance so maybe that was a good sign.

As the trooper walked towards him, he stepped out of the car. "Is Alice okay? Can I go talk to her please?"

"Sir, I need you to get back in your car. Help is on the way, but perhaps it would be better for you to wait at home. We will have someone come speak with you shortly."

"I don't understand. The accident doesn't appear to be too bad."

"Mr. Myers, please go home. Your wife is not here. We are bringing in the dogs and the crime scene techs."

Jack went pale. "I don't understand. Where could she be? It's not like her just to walk away, especially from the scene of an accident."

"It could be that she was out of sorts and went looking for help."

"But she has a cell phone. She would've just used it to call 911."

"Yes sir. Her cell phone was under the passenger seat.
Maybe she panicked when she couldn't find it. The
dogs will help us find out which direction she took off
in."

Jack had a distinct impression the state trooper was
holding something back. More cops were arriving on
scene. The canine unit had arrived as well as the crime
scene techs. Jack wondered why the crime scene unit
would be needed for a car accident. Where was Alice?
Was she okay? The dogs were sniffing the car but did
not take off in any direction. When the FBI task force
made its appearance, Jack became extremely worried.
On TV, the canine always would catch a scent and take
off. Instead, the dogs simply circled the car.

A cop approached his car. "Mr. Myers, my name is
Sheriff Matthews. I'm the Sheriff in Hope, Louisiana. I
don't mean to worry you sir but we fear your wife may
have been kidnapped. Would it be possible for us to
listen to your wife's voicemail? We would also like to
have it analyzed by a specialist for other noises we
might be missing. We want to try to bring your wife
home as soon as possible."

Jack had gone white. "Hope, Louisiana? Isn't that the
town in the news lately? Wait, didn't the papers
report something about a serial killer? Oh God in
heaven please no."

"Mr. Myers we are not jumping to any conclusions just
yet. We are looking into all possibilities. Please let me
have someone drive you home. We will make sure

someone brings you your car. Also, please give us a call if your wife does call you or comes home. We will post an officer at your house just in case."

Chapter 98

St. Anthony's Cemetery had been located on the outskirts of town for over a century. Many family plots and several vaults were on the premises. The wrought iron fence went all the way around the cemetery. There were several large stone cherubs near the entrance. There were also some very large oak trees placed strategically in the cemetery to make sure they didn't disturb the poor souls resting in everlasting peace.

Thankfully the cemetery hadn't had the same problems as those in New Orleans. No flooding problems here, which meant no poor bodies floating away. Unfortunately, with the economy as it was, the grave robbers had become a problem.

Unbeknownst to the general public, small cameras were placed at the entryways and in strategic points around the cemetery. They were hidden and were working properly. Solar lights were placed on the grave sites to give a soft illumination at each site. At night you could see the soft blue hues throughout. At least it kept the cemetery from being bathed in complete darkness at night. Although, it did give off an eerie glow. The moonlight fell on the life-size angel statues on several of the older graves and gave them an ethereal look.

***

The Hunter entered the graveyard cautiously. This masterpiece should be left hanging for all to enjoy. A big funeral was scheduled tomorrow morning so there would be a large audience to appreciate his work. It was too bad she couldn't hold out a day. She just didn't have the fight in her or perhaps the excitement of the accident had set him off.

He threw the rope over the branch. Next he created a noose and wrapped it under her arms. He hauled the body up and secured the rope around the trunk of the tree. She resembled merely another angel in the cemetery. He wanted her to face his family plot. His mom and dad would finally see one of his masterpieces up close and personal. He wondered if his Detective would put it together. He pulled the ball cap a little lower and headed back to the van. It was time to go back home.

***

The funeral home workers arrived at the cemetery early that morning. There was a chance of rain and they wanted a tent and chairs set up for the family by the graveside. As they neared the site, they noticed something dangling from the tree. The men immediately called 911 and the funeral home director.

They knew not to get too close but what could a few pictures hurt? What with all the reporters crawling all over town surely someone would be interested in buying photos of the latest victim of the elusive serial killer. The men thought about the money they could make.

Cops swarmed the place in no time. The men informed

them what time they had arrived. They didn't notice anyone around when they got there. They never noticed anything out of the ordinary, except, of course, the body.

The manager of the cemetery immediately sought out Sheriff Matthews as soon as she arrived.   Now she was glad they had installed the security cameras. Maybe they would catch a glimpse of the murdering psychopath.

"Sheriff Matthews, may I speak with you please?   You may not be aware of this but we do have security cameras at the entryway and in various places throughout the cemetery."

Her comment caught Sheriff Matthews off guard. "Wait. What? Are they working?" He gave her a dumbfounded expression for a moment as he considered what she'd said. Did they finally catch a break? "Well then, let's go take a look at those tapes shall we?"

"Right this way. The monitors are in the back office. We still haven't hired a security guard. After last night, one will be hired though. Unfortunately, now I can justify twenty-four hour surveillance. First the grave robbers and now this.   What else could happen?" Sitting at the desk she told him, "Let me rewind these tapes and see what we have. This system also has an automatic backup so we could get you a copy for your records."

Sheriff Matthews said a Hail Mary as the recording

went back in time. "Let's start at midnight."

Nothing.   It wasn't until 2 a.m. when he saw the white van pull up. Excitement bubbled up inside him. The fibers from the first victim and the glass from Alice Myers's accident were suspected to be from a Ford van.

"Please be our guy. Let's hope we can make out a company logo, or better yet a license number."

As the van drove through the gates the company logo, TeleCall, came into view. A few seconds later the license plate came in plain sight.

Sheriff Matthews called dispatch. "We have the SOB. I want a BOLO out immediately for a white van with the TeleCall logo. The license plate number is TOW397. We may have this psycho captured before the end of the day."

They watched anxiously as the figure stepped out of the vehicle. At first it was dark and hard to make the person out. That was until he moved to the back of the van.

Sheriff Matthews was stunned. "That is David Thorguson. His family has a hunting camp here. They resided in Springport. David Sr. grew up here. His family resided here for years in the house, if that is what you could call it. Now it is strictly a hunting camp. David's mother and father passed away in a tragic car accident several years ago."

                                   ***

The Hunter noticed a roadblock up ahead. He figured
it was a routine checkpoint, possibly checking for
insurance or inspection stickers. Nothing for him to
worry about. He was in a hurry to get out of town,
back to his home in Springport. He wanted to watch
the early addition of the news. This time he was sure
his masterpiece would be shown.

He had everything ready as he approached the state
trooper.   Before he realized what was going on, a swat
team had the van surrounded.

"What the hell is going on?" He shouted out the
window. There was no way they could possibly know it
was him. He had been extremely careful except for the
car accident and there had been no witnesses. Had
the bitch managed to call the accident in?

"We have you surrounded. Please exit the vehicle
carefully with both hands up in the air."

The Hunter did as he was ordered.

The state trooper called Sheriff Matthews
immediately. "We have David Thorguson in custody.
They are bringing him in now."

                                   ***

Sheriff Matthews let out a sigh of relief. They still had
to interrogate David. Someone also had to notify Alice
Myers's husband of her unfortunate death. He could

also inform the other victims' family members that the murderer had been caught. It was time to let the victims rest in peace.

The FBI wanted to conduct the interview. Sheriff Matthews agreed wholeheartedly with the idea. Alex was considered a specialist in this field and would handle the interview. He had interviewed several serial killers whereas Sheriff Matthews has never seen the likes of a crime like this. He prayed he never would again.

For the time being, David Thorguson was cooling his heels in a jail cell. The police station was small and they didn't have a true interrogation room. The FBI would arrange a temporary interrogation room for the time being. It would take some time though. David Thorguson would eventually be transferred to Springport Prison. They handled the most hardened criminals there. A public defender had been called in for David for now. They wanted to make sure he wouldn't be released on any technicalities, although David wasn't talking at all currently. He sat in the cell with a blank look on his face.

***

Alex was certain there were more victims than just those that David displayed. Someone didn't just start out killing and displaying the bodies. The killings were almost ritualistic in the murderer's mind. Alex had always been good at what he did but profiling could not be considered an exact science. There were too many variables to take into consideration.

Interviewing the serial killer helped him to get inside the mind of future serial killers. These killers were becoming better each time at dodging forensics, leaving behind little to no clues which made capturing them even more difficult. All of these women died such horrific deaths. The latest victim had been the worst.

The autopsy reports revealed a possibility that he had sexual intercourse with the bodies even after death. At first, the burn marks were thought to be a form of a cigarette but now it looked to be from a butane torch. A search warrant was being processed for the van, his residence and camp. This should help answer more questions.

Alex profiled David Thorguson as a narcissist. No one had informed Mr. Thorguson as to what led to his capture. No one had spoken to him yet and he hadn't said a word since his capture. Even without David speaking to them, he had a demeanor about him. He truly believed he was intellectually above the police. There would be no denying he was a completely functioning psychopath.

Alex believed that somewhere down the line a woman hurt David so he decided to take his anger out on all females.

Chapter 99

David was still in a holding cell at the sheriff's office until the lawyer arrived. They would be moving him in the next day or so to the local jail, and then he knew it wouldn't be long before they actually sent him up to Springport Prison.

He quickly became agitated. The walls were closing in on him and the tiny room reeked of urine. He continuously paced back and forth in this tiny cell. He heard the news reporter talking on the TV about the latest murder and a suspect was in custody. How did they catch him so fast?   He had been so careful to make sure he left no forensic evidence behind, there was never a witness. How the hell did they catch him?

While pacing, he relived each of his hunts in his head. The anticipation of the hunt and the exhilaration of the kill. Where did he go wrong? He had to get out of here. He had to be free; free to hunt and free to kill.

The sheriff and his lackeys were going to the Hideaway in the morning. All his secrets would be revealed when they searched his house or camp. They would find the DVDs. He would fry for sure. He had to get out of here and destroy everything.

Chapter 100

Sheriff Matthews, Agent Hamilton, an FBI forensics team, and the state troopers' crime scene techs were all at David Thorguson's hunting camp, The Hideaway, at daybreak. At first glance, it was charming when you drove up to it. The leaves were all gone from the crêpe myrtle trees lining the drive, but come spring it would be beautiful.

The Hideaway had an unmistakable aura about it. Sheriff Matthews knew right away this was where the women were tortured and murdered. The aura surrounding the place was reminiscent to a cemetery but these poor souls weren't at peace. The presence of death resonated here.

A cypress swing hung on the back porch overlooking the bayou. The electricity and plumbing were in serious need of an update, but after the horrific murders committed here, Sheriff Matthews didn't foresee this place ever selling. No one in their right mind would want to own a camp where true evil was once present.

The crime scene techs moved their mobile unit out here and were in the process of setting it up. There would be a lot of evidence to process. They were about to enter the cabin itself.

The camp had gleaming wood walls and flooring. It was actually spotless. It was hard to believe a bachelor lived here, especially a psychotic one.

The FBI brought in ground penetrating radar to search for buried bodies. The crime scene unit found where David Thorguson hid his DVD's. David recorded each and every kill he ever committed. There were over two dozen of them. It would take someone with a strong stomach to watch them.

The furnishings in the cabin were grander than Sheriff Matthews expected. The Thorgusons had very good taste. The living room furnishings consisted of a leather sectional with built in recliners. A gorgeous electric fireplace in the corner with a massive plasma TV perched on top. The dining room was furnished with an antique dining set.

The cabin appeared small on the outside but it was actually quite roomy on the inside. The master bedroom consisted of a king sized, antique pineapple bed with an antique bureau. The TV and DVD player were hidden in an armoire. A gun closet was tucked into the back of the bedroom closet as well as a large trunk with more torture devices. A now outdated bathroom had been added to the master bedroom years ago.

"Sheriff, you should see this." As the sheriff entered the room, it reeked of bleach and death. The ceiling and walls were covered in mirrors. In the center of the room sat what once was an OB/GYN chair or dental chair, possibly even the two combined. It was definitely retrofitted for torture. Just looking around the room confirmed that the sick fucker liked to watch himself kill.

What once must have been David's room growing up had been transformed into his "play" room. Inside the closet was a strange shackle device that not only held the head in place, but there were several latches going up the whole length to restrain the captive's arms and legs. It had been retrofitted and welded onto an old time iron bedspring. Was this possibly some kind of homemade iron maiden? You could clearly see the springs had been sharpened. If you leaned back, blood would be drawn.

The mirrors also explained why the girl's eyes were pried open; he forced them to watch. They also noticed the camera set up in the corner of the room. He managed to record each of his killings. There was enough evidence here to bury him under the jail. David Thorguson would never see the light of day again. Maybe he would do everyone a favor and plead out. It sure would save the town the cost of an expensive trial.

Sheriff Matthews couldn't remember how many pots of coffee he had drank so far. They had been processing the camp for several hours now. They were nowhere near done. They reviewed several DVD's of the torture and murder of numerous women for over 3 hours. Everyone agreed in unison to stop for the day. No one had the stomach to watch more.

The media camped out at the main road hoping to get closer. So far the deputies had been successful at keeping out everyone that didn't belong.

Sheriff Matthews often wondered the importance of cutting the women's breasts off until he saw them in the freezer. David had bitten the areola area and left perfect dental impressions.

***

David Thorguson was the epitome of evil. Jordan's mind kept drifting back to the victims' families. Her mother used to say time heals all wounds. She didn't foresee time healing these wounds though. Children were going to grow up without a mother, husbands cut short on their time with their wife, holiday time would be remembered as the time the victim died a brutal unspeakable death.

She still had nightmares about the bodies. She could only imagine what the victims' loved ones were going through.

The men had somber looks on their faces as the bodies were uncovered. Five grave sites had been carefully dug up. Fifteen bodies had been found. The bastard buried three bodies in each grave. They were just tossed in like yesterday's garbage. He didn't care for these women even after death. Each and every woman would need to be identified. David's treasure chest had been discovered. Several purses were found in a closet. The belongings were being sorted through. Hopefully this would help with identification.

They also found an assortment of whips in a closet. Some had razor blades applied to them while others had stones that had been cut and sharpened. Each was meant to bring pain and draw blood. There were also several instruments lying out on a table that appeared to have just been cleaned and left to air dry.

David's bedroom smelled of body odor and sweat. The nightstand had a stack of S&M porno magazines. There were even more under the bed. Besides the DVD collection David made, they found several snuff films. What possessed someone to make these types of films? There were truly some sick minds in this world.

The victims' families' lives had been shattered. They were left trying to pick up the pieces, but with David Thorguson finally caught they could get some justice. They would also get some closure.

Everyone was tired and hungry. They wanted something more than the sandwiches that had been brought out. They needed something stronger to drink than coffee. They'd all had a long and tedious day of going through the camp. Crime scene tape was put up and a couple of deputies would stay at the gate to keep out onlookers and the press.

Night was closing in on them. They would continue the search tomorrow. Thankfully the land only consisted of four acres. Hopefully no more bodies would turn up.

***

Sheriff Matthews looked out at the bayou. It resembled a black hole. There was no breeze, no ripples in the water and completely lifeless. It had an eerie feeling about it. You could feel the horrors that happened here at night, all the deaths it had witnessed through the years.

Moss had started growing on the crepe myrtle trees. With the sun setting it resembled witch's hair blowing in the breeze from the skeletal branches of the trees. It gave the driveway a truly wicked feeling. To complete the eerie feeling, when the wind blew through the trees it sounded like moans. Yep, this place was definitely eerie at night.

The death penalty was too good for David Thorguson. It was too bad they couldn't go back to the biblical times where an eye for an eye, tooth for a tooth justice prevailed. David Thorguson was the epitome of true evil and deserved to be punished.

There was a pretty good chance that he would become someone's bitch in prison. If he even lasted long at all. Prisoners tended to hand out justice of their own.

The cocky SOB still refused to talk to them. Instead, he merely stared at them blankly. He refused to say anything. They had David Thorguson by the balls finally and yet he still had the upper hand. Only he knew how many poor girls he killed and hopefully their names.

Sheriff Matthews felt as if this case aged him by several years. His body was starting to show the signs of being straddled behind the desk. He also had the beginnings of a beer gut and his once full head of hair showed signs of thinning. He was surprised this case didn't make him completely bald by now. At 58 he believed he stilled looked good. He had no idea why his wife had stayed with him all these years. She had to put up with a lot these last few months too. Mindy was a good woman though.

Chapter 101

The public defender finally made his appearance. He sat in an office waiting for a deputy to bring David to meet with him. He knew this was an open and shut case. The sheriff and FBI profiler were anxious to speak with David but they had to wait. First, he needed to speak with David. This case could catapult his career or end it. There was absolutely no way the guy was getting off but maybe he could get the death penalty lifted.

"David, my name is Douglas Powell. I've been assigned to represent you. Have you been read your rights?"

"Yes, I have. I just don't understand how I ended up here."

"David, truth be told, you murdered several women. The evidence so far is pretty damning. I'm going to at least try to get the death penalty off the table. Maybe plead insanity."

"What evidence could they possibly have?"

"Well, David, you see the cemetery had surveillance cameras set up. They never made that fact public knowledge. It turns out they were having a problem with grave robbers. They never expected to catch you in the act.

"The surveillance tape led to your arrest and a search warrant has been issued for your property. The DVD's have been found. Ground penetrating radar has been finding the bodies all day that were buried on your property. They also found several purses, cell phones, articles of clothing, and jewelry belonging to the women. Right now a task force is trying to identify the bodies.

"This is where my leverage will come into play. If you agree to assist them with identifying those you have killed I am going to ask that they take the death penalty off the table. I also plan on asking for a lesser sentence by pleading mental incapacity."

David was enraged. "A fucking surveillance camera on the cemetery grounds! That's how those imbeciles caught me? I want to speak with the FBI. I want to shove it in all of their faces that I outsmarted them this whole time. I will gladly give them the names of all the lives I took. Just one thing, I want a book written about me. I want it well known how many of those stupid women I killed and how I had the police outsmarted for so long. I want to be immortalized. I refuse to plead insanity you hear. I had them chasing their tails."

The attorney may be young, but he looked slick. He was impeccably dressed for a small town lawyer. He watched David's expressions like a hawk. Just by talking with him, David could tell he wasn't going to try to get him off. No, that would ruin his career. Especially with all the evidence against him. This small town would make sure he never worked here again if that happened.

David still couldn't believe that he wanted him to plead

insanity. That would not happen. David wasn't insane.

***

After David finished speaking with his attorney, he returned to the damned cell. Now he had to wait for Sheriff Matthews to return. He was losing his mind locked up in here. He found it difficult to breath.

While sitting in his cell, David had plenty of time to ponder his childhood. If only people knew what happened behind closed doors, that his childhood happiness had been superficial. David could remember his mother holding his hand when he was nine and smiling but her eyes were always vacant and sad.

He reminisced his first kill while hunting with his dad. He had been eight and they had gone deer hunting. David managed to kill a ten point buck. The exhilaration of the kill became overwhelming when his dad smeared the blood on his face after the kill. The feel and taste sent a rush of excitement through him. The hunting, or killing to be more precise, was in his blood after that. David couldn't wait to leave Springport and go hunting. As he grew older, killing animals didn't hold the same excitement.

His dad had been one of the top defense lawyers at the firm. David paid close attention to everything his dad said when he talked about work. Not to become the perfect lawyer, but the perfect criminal. His dad enjoyed talking about how these criminals ended up in jail because of their stupid, careless mistakes.

David knew his soul was evil. His grandmother constantly called him the demon's spawn. Maybe he was, after all his dad was a mean son of a bitch. He had never been a loving and caring parent. He was downright mean to his mom. What bothered David the most was she just took his abuse. The only time his dad wasn't a mean SOB was out at the camp.

His dad never seemed to talk to his mom; instead, he always yelled or talked down to her. At night you could hear the slaps sounding like a whip cracking through the air. The stupid bitch, she would just let his dad do as he pleased. Women were stupid, weak, and pathetic. They were no better than the animals he hunted.

His dad considered David useless, a waste of space on this planet. He constantly informed David he would never be good at anything but hunting, and that he had his doubts about him. Nope, David didn't miss his parents one bit.

No one had ever been the wiser that his parents were his first kill. David started killing women right after his parents' funeral. It gave him a new sense of freedom. There wouldn't be anyone out at the camp. Those that had fought back, he had more "fun" with.   The women's fear fed his adrenaline and heightened the exhilaration of the kill.

Chapter 102

David Thorguson was more disturbing and twisted than they ever imagined. What those women must have experienced. Even in his worst nightmares Sheriff Matthews never would have thought what these women endured was humanly possible.

Agent Hamilton suspected that David had had a dark side for a very long time. Some serial killers show psychopathic tendencies as children. David always appeared to be a quiet kid, but instead he harbored a darker side than anyone would have ever guessed.

Sheriff Matthews still couldn't believe the killer turned out to be David Thorguson. He never thought David had any ambition in life. *Cet homme-ça a jamais travaillé un jour de sa vie.* That man there never worked a day in his life!

The capture of David Thorguson brought instant national media coverage. Even more television and print journalists continued to arrive in Hope. It brought a booming business to the local restaurants and bed and breakfast inns. This was not the kind of popularity the mayor ever wanted for Hope.

The road leading to David Thorguson's camp had become the command post for all the media. Nothing was sacred to them.

Sheriff Matthews surveyed the area around the cabin. It was daybreak and a gentle breeze was blowing. The treetops were swaying. If he didn't think about what had transpired here it could be a relaxing morning. He heard a creature rustling in the woods. The deer saw all the commotion and took off. The wildlife wasn't used to this much human interaction out here. Until now, he never considered just how perfect this place was to kidnap and torture someone. There was no one around.

Jordan walked up to Sheriff Matthews and said, "The size of David Thorguson's ego amazes me. Even after being caught he still thinks he has us all by the balls."

"Unfortunately he does at this time. We are only just beginning to find out how many women he has killed. Only he knows their names, or at least I pray he does."

She stared out at the bayou. "If only the bayou could tell the secrets it knows." The bayou could be a tempting mistress at times. It had been to many men over the years, but it kept its secrets hidden deep below in its dark, murky waters.

The camp was no longer a crime scene, but it would always be where the gruesome murders took place. No matter how well it was cleaned up, the horrors of what happened here could never be erased. This camp would probably stay unoccupied in years to come.

Chapter 103

A huge weight had been lifted off of everyone's shoulders. Sheriff Matthews suggested everyone meet at Rosy's to celebrate.

"Let's get out of here and actually enjoy a supper. I'm buying."

Johnson joked, "Well, in that case I'm ordering the filet and crab cakes."

"Son, you can get whatever you want. The town is picking up the tab. I'm thinking we need to have a traditional fais-do-do to celebrate once this is all done. Have the whole town dance the night away."

Over dinner they talked more about David Thorguson. The sheriff informed Alex, "David didn't go to school here. I think his dad thought he was too good to go to school here actually. Even though we do have a very good private school and the public school is one of the best in the state. David's family actually lived in Springport. His family would come on weekends and holidays. My parents grew up with David Sr. When he became a lawyer he moved to the city. He made it big there. Dad said David Sr. always wanted more money, no matter how much he had it was never enough. He didn't like growing up poor and he despised hanging out with the poor or middle class kids. He always had his sights set on bigger and better things. Dad thinks the only reason he kept the place was to rub it in the town's face that he had finally made it. He had a look at me now attitude."

Johnson went on to say, "David's parents were killed in an auto accident a few years back. No one knows for sure exactly what happened. They died on impact as well as the driver in the other vehicle. David Sr. had been drinking, but that wasn't unusual."

"My dad always had a suspicion David Sr. had a drinking problem. The other driver was drunk also." Jordan continued, "David was an only child so everything went to him. He's not a bad looking man. Average, but he wouldn't turn any heads. He wasn't the type of man that would have women fighting over him. He had one of those faces you wouldn't remember in a crowd. He always kept to himself, kind of a loner. If you could get him to talk, he always seemed sweet but quiet. I remember his favorite thing to talk about was hunting. It seemed as if his life revolved around it.

"Dad always suspected abuse, but he could never prove it. He said if he was wrong it would have been a career ender for all those involved in the accusations."

Alex looked over at Jordan, "Enough talk about David Thorguson, let's enjoy the rest of our night. Tomorrow is going to be a busy day."

Jordan couldn't agree more, she wanted to enjoy whatever time she had remaining with Alex

***

After dinner, Alex met up with Jordan at her house.

Kissing her greedily he stated, "I should be working on my interview with David tomorrow."

Now that David had been captured, Jordan knew that Alex would be leaving soon. She wanted to take advantage of every minute he was here.

"Mm mmm, don't say that name. It tends to kill the mood."

She undressed him as she spoke. Dropping to her knees she placed butterfly kisses all over his lower body. He was rock hard.

"You're killing me. That's driving me absolutely crazy. I'm never going to get any work done."

Greedily she took him in her mouth. He had to pull her away. He took her hard, no time for foreplay. After his release he caressed and touched her all over.

"I wasn't exactly fair to you. Now it's my turn to make you lose your mind. I'm going to keep you in orgasmic pleasure."

Alex was so different from the other men she had dated. She was not ready for the day that Alex had to leave.

****

Alex felt that Jordan should sit in with him during the interview. Maybe it would trip David up some, might make him a little more uncomfortable. The hate that David felt for women was apparent. Although they had more than enough evidence, her being present in the room may be enough to push him over the edge. They still needed the names of the victims found buried on the property.

Sheriff Matthews entered the makeshift interrogation room with them and started the introductions, "David Thorguson and Douglas Powell, this is Detective Jordan Sanders and FBI Agent Alex Hamilton."

David leered at Detective Sanders with a hunger in his eyes.

"So you're the FBI profiler?" He asked while never taking his eyes off *mon douce* Detective.

"I am. I want to talk to you. Sheriff Matthews has another pressing matter so Detective Sanders will fill in for him."

Alex looked at David, "Before we get into the kidnapping and murders, I would like to try to understand you a little better. Did your parents love you? Were they good parents?"

"Let's just say when they died, there was no love lost."

Chapter 104

The DA knew this trial would be open and shut. He was looking forward to this trial and actually hoped that David Thorguson and his attorney didn't take the plea deal on the table. He already had his closing argument written. They had more than enough evidence now. Jurors loved open and shut cases. Jurors wanted to get in and out of the courthouse as fast as they could. They no longer cared about their civic duty. Cases with as much evidence as they had would keep jurors from feeling guilty about sentencing this man to death. The death penalty was too good for this man.

David Thorguson's attorney was trying to push the criminally insane card. Which rarely worked. David Thorguson refused to let his attorney play that card. The man swore that he was competent. The brutality of these murders was so severe though that the DA wondered how competent Thorguson actually was. Thorguson had no problem letting you know he was proud of these murders. He called them his masterpieces. He had an incredibly inflated ego. The DA and FBI Agent Hamilton both wanted to take that ego down a notch or two.

There was such savagery in these murders. David Thorguson showed sheer boldness in his abductions and disposals of these victims that Agent Hamilton couldn't wait to interview him. However, David Thorguson continued to act as if he had the upper hand in the matter. Perhaps he did, only David Thorguson knew how many women he'd actually murdered. Plus, they still had bodies to identify. David wanted praise and recognition for all that he had done. The SOB even wanted a book written about him glorifying the work he did.

Chapter 105

Sheriff Matthews was glad this case was over. This was the biggest case him or his deputies had ever had. Hopefully this would be the first and last. He looked at the murder board in dismay. So many lives had been taken away, families destroyed.

Much to the DA's dismay, Thorguson took the plea deal, of course with several stipulations. Much to everyone's frustration, the death penalty was taken off of the table. Agent Hamilton elected to take a sabbatical and agreed to write the book about David Thorguson with the stipulation that Alex would write the book as he saw fit and how any money made would be disbursed. He also would be allowed to study David Thorguson for further research on serial killers.

David Thorguson didn't have all the names of his victims, but did remember where each and every one was abducted from. This helped to locate missing person's reports in those areas. It would still be a long and tedious process.

***

The more Alex thought about it, the more he wanted to study this killer's mind. It may help in the capture of future serial killers. The book had the potential to be a money maker, but the money should not go to David Thorguson. The money should help the families left behind.

Plus, Alex wasn't sure he could leave Jordan. He'd

never felt this way about a woman before. He wondered if she felt the same way about him.

Alex suspected that a civil suit would be brought against David Thorguson right after the verdict was given. The victims' families would be awarded everything David had.

Chapter 106

Sheriff Matthews looked at himself in the mirror. He no longer recognized himself. This case had taken a toll on him. Thank heavens the monster was finally caught. If it wouldn't have been for the cemetery and those cameras there was no telling how long this would have gone on.

Election time was right around the corner. He had talked it over with his wife, and he was ready to retire and she was ready for him to be home more. He would back Jordan if she wanted to run for sheriff.

"Jordan, can you come into my office?"

"Yes sir, you wanted to see me?"

"I'm sure you've heard the rumors. I have decided to retire. This case was more than I ever wanted in my career. You handled yourself well. If you want to run for sheriff, I will back you one hundred percent. I am positive I can get the mayor on board also."

***

Jordan was dumbfounded. She didn't know what to say. Sheriff Matthew's statement astounded her. She always wanted to be a cop, it was in her blood. She was also very ambitious and thought being sheriff was what she wanted. That was before she met Alex, though. Now she wasn't sure what she wanted.

"Sir, you will be deeply missed. If I run, I have some

very hard shoes to fill."

"Think about it and let me know. You have a bit of time before nominees are named."

This was a lot for her to absorb. Alex was talking about taking a sabbatical and living here while writing a book on David Thorguson's life. Jordan couldn't be happier with that news. They were still unsure what the future held; only time would tell. Now, she may have a chance to run for sheriff. She couldn't wait to see Alex at the house tonight and discuss all the possibilities with him.

www.ingramcontent.com/pod-product-compliance
Lightning Source LLC
Chambersburg PA
CBHW070745190726
48292CB00002B/419